WILD HEART

paige press

WILD HEART

NEW YORK TIMES BESTSELLING AUTHOR
LAURELIN PAIGE

ALSO BY LAURELIN PAIGE

Visit my website for a more detailed reading order.

The Dirty Universe

Dirty Filthy Rich Boys - READ FREE

Dirty Duet (Donovan Kincaid)

Dirty Filthy Rich Men | Dirty Filthy Rich Love

Kincaid (coming 2022)

Dirty Games Duet (Weston King)

Dirty Sexy Player| Dirty Sexy Games

Dirty Sweet Duet (Dylan Locke)

Sweet Liar | Sweet Fate

(Nate Sinclair) Dirty Filthy Fix (a spinoff novella)

Dirty Wild Trilogy (Cade Warren)

Wild Rebel | Wild War | Wild Heart

Man in Charge Duet

Man in Charge

Man in Love

Man for Me (a spinoff novella)

The Fixed Universe

Fixed Series (Hudson & Alayna)

Fixed on You | Found in You | Forever with You | Hudson | Fixed Forever

Found Duet (Gwen & JC) Free Me | Find Me

(Chandler & Genevieve) Chandler (a spinoff novella)

(Norma & Boyd) Falling Under You (a spinoff novella)

(Nate & Trish) Dirty Filthy Fix (a spinoff novella)

Slay Series (Celia & Edward)

Rivalry | Ruin | Revenge | Rising

(Gwen & JC) The Open Door (a spinoff novella)

(Camilla & Hendrix) Slash (a spinoff novella)

First and Last

First Touch | Last Kiss

Hollywood Standalones

One More Time

Close

Sex Symbol

Star Struck

Dating Season

Spring Fling | Summer Rebound | Fall Hard

Winter Bloom | Spring Fever | Summer Lovin

Also written with Kayti McGee under the name Laurelin McGee

Miss Match | Love Struck | MisTaken | Holiday for Hire

Written with Sierra Simone

Porn Star | Hot Cop

Be sure to **sign up for my newsletter** where you'll receive **a FREE book every month** from bestselling authors, only available to my subscribers, as well as up-to-date information on my latest releases.

PRO TIP: Add laurelin@laurelinpaige.com to your contacts before signing up to be sure the list comes right to your inbox.

DID YOU KNOW...

This book is available in both paperback and audiobook editions at all major online retailers! Links are on my website. If you'd like to order a signed paperback, my online store is open several times a year here.

ONE
JOLIE

Past

THE SOFT LANDING of something on my upper back woke me up. I opened my eyes and rolled over to discover my father towering over me and a grocery bag on the bed behind me. I didn't have to look inside to know what I'd find.

"You know what to do." He handed me an empty plastic cup.

I stifled a groan, and simultaneously, I felt my stomach drop. Stuffing down my emotions often led to a sense of dread, but this was more than that. While the routine was familiar to me, I had real reason to fear today's results would be different.

I'd been trying not to think about that. I wouldn't be able to push it off now.

Out of habit, my gaze flickered to my window. He'd glued it

shut the day after he'd discovered Cade in my room. He'd installed bars the following week, sealing me in a literal prison.

How long ago had that been now? Four weeks? Only four more until he came back for me. It already felt like a lifetime had passed, and graduation day seemed an eternity away.

"Hurry it up, Julianna. I need to be in early for a meeting with Sylvia."

No wonder my alarm hadn't gone off yet.

With a sigh, I threw the covers off me and picked up the bag. "We did this just two weeks ago," I said, but I swung my legs around and put my feet on the floor. Complaining about it wouldn't get me out of it.

"When you behave like a whore, you should expect to be treated like one."

My empty stomach churned, and I wondered if I could manage to throw up on his shoe if I angled myself right.

But the wave of nausea passed, so with the grocery bag in one hand and the cup in the other, I headed to the bathroom.

"Leave the door propped open," he reminded me when I tried to close it out of habit.

This wasn't new either. He always made me keep the door ajar, as though he thought I might have urine tucked away somewhere in my bathroom cabinets, and I'd try to substitute it out for mine. And even if I did, what good would that do?

It wasn't really about what I might do, though. It was about control. It was about me understanding that he was my lord and master. My prison guard. The person who controlled my fate.

What would he do when I ran away?

I almost wished I could be there to see his reaction.

A smile briefly bent my lips thinking about it, but it

vanished as soon as I took the cardboard box out of the bag, and I was forced to face my situation. This was the whole reason I'd avoided truly fantasizing about the future with Cade this last week. This unknown could change everything, and I hadn't been able to process that possibility.

"Julianna?" My father was as impatient to get this over with as I was reluctant.

"Sorry. I was rereading the instructions." It was a lie that was hard to justify considering how often I'd had to take these —once a month since I'd started my period, more frequently since he'd caught me with Cade—but I noisily tore into the box so he wouldn't feel the need to confront me on it.

Leaving the unpackaged stick on the counter, I took the cup with me to the toilet to do the deed. "This would really be easier if you just put me on the pill. Since you're so worried about me getting knocked up."

This was another familiar conversation, and he didn't even bother to give me his usual lecture about how preparation was an invitation and all that.

That wasn't the reason he didn't give me protection. It was another way he could control me. Plus, I was pretty sure he got off on how humiliating the whole thing was. *Sick fuck.*

I flushed the toilet and took the cup, now filled with my pee, back to the bathroom counter. After uncapping the stick, I dipped the end in and counted to ten. Then I put the cap back on and set it on the counter while I washed my hands, trying to ignore the current wave of nausea and the probability that I didn't need this test to know what was going on inside me.

As soon as he heard the sound of the faucet, my father nudged the door the rest of the way open and leaned against the frame.

His eyes were pinned to the test, watching as the pink control line brightened. "You know what happens if this is positive, right?"

This was another speech he gave every time. He would take me to the doctor to get me an abortion. I'd go through the procedure willingly, or he'd tie me to the bed and take care of it himself with a hanger if need be. There would be no bastard grandchild. End of story.

I couldn't bear to hear it this time. "Yes, I know."

"Are you sure? Maybe you should tell me so I can be sure you're clear."

"I know, Dad," I snapped. "I don't need to repeat it back to you."

His eyes darkened, and his hand twitched at his side while he tried to decide what to do about my disrespect. It was obvious he wanted to backhand me, and I wasn't sure why he even had to think about it since he rarely denied himself a reason to punish me, especially since the whole Cade incident. He'd been taking out his wrath about that on me for the past month.

Today, though, he let it go and glanced at his watch. "One more minute."

One more minute until the truth was confirmed. One more minute until I could no longer pretend my breasts didn't hurt more than when they did with PMS and that my exhaustion wasn't just about missing Cade and my missed period wasn't about stress and that the come-and-go nausea wasn't a weird stomach bug.

What if I was? What would I do then?

Tears pricked, and I shut my eyes, refusing to watch for the second line. I had forty-five seconds left before I had to figure anything out, and I planned on putting it off as long as possible.

My eyes were still closed when I heard my father move to pick up the stick from the counter. "How likely is it his?"

A sob threatened in my chest—or another urge to vomit—and I had to sit down on the edge of the bathtub for support. He knew the answer already, but he wanted me to know it too, and even though I already did, I did the math, figured out the calendar in my head, and thought about when I was most likely ovulating.

The thing was, I didn't know.

And there was no way I could know without a paternity test, and I didn't know if that was even possible before a baby was born, which meant I couldn't have an abortion, no matter what my father said. I wouldn't give up Cade's child. No way, no how.

But being pregnant put a wrench in running away with Cade. And if it ended up not being his, was it fair to saddle him with that burden?

"You need money to have a child," my father said, as if he could read my mind. "You need a home. Insurance. Healthcare. Baby clothes and furniture. Who's going to pay for diapers? And formula? Minimum wage isn't going to get you far. Even if you're both working."

I wasn't surprised that he had guessed I'd been planning to leave. I pushed him off every time he tried to talk about my plans after graduation, and he'd made it very clear he wanted me to stay with him while I got a degree in education so I could come help out at the family school.

What did surprise me was something else. "You'll let me keep it?"

He set the stick on the counter and came to crouch in front of me so we were eye to eye. He had his doting father mask on, which was probably the cruelest of all his masks because it confused me and tore at my emotions. "It will be very hard," he said softly, taking my hands in his. "And you'll need my support, but if that's what you really want, princess, of course you can keep it."

Silent tears streamed down my cheeks. I had no options. It was a facade of a choice.

So I took the devil's bargain, knowing full well that nothing he offered came without a cost.

TWO
JOLIE

Present

I PUSHED OPEN the front door and blinked, as if closing my eyes could make the boy and his duffel bag go away, but he was still very much there, standing in the yard when I opened them. "Tate?"

"Ah. There. My mom," he said to Cade, who was standing next to him with a look of horror on his face that had to match my own.

Immediately, the air went out of my lungs. The doorknob under my hand felt sweaty, and my heart was racing so fast and so hard, it felt like a trapped animal inside my chest.

This can't be happening.

After Cade left the room, I must have rolled over and fallen back to sleep, and now I was dreaming. There was no other explanation. Because the scene in front of me was plucked directly from my worst nightmare, and no way was it really happening.

The current dread was such a contrast from how I'd been floating on air only a few minutes before. Cade had promised he would see this through with my father, and maybe that was more about his own relationship with Dad, but I could tell things were changing. I could feel the tether between us—the one that had always been there, had never broken even when we'd been apart—and instead of yanking at it, trying to break free like he had earlier in the week, it had started to feel like he was shortening the leash, pulling me closer.

And I was ready to stop resisting being pulled.

I was ready to tell him everything, and that felt pretty damn good.

With the truth on my mind, I'd thought of Tate and reached for my phone. It had been a while since I'd checked in on him, and even though I knew he was mature enough to handle being alone with the neighbor keeping an eye on him, I still got anxious when I didn't hear from him for too long.

The fact that my phone wasn't anywhere in the room demonstrated just how distracted I'd been in my old home. Had I really not texted Tate since dinner? Panicking before it was necessary, I'd jumped out of bed and thrown on a change of clothes so I could go look for it.

Then, when I'd come downstairs, the sound of an engine drew my gaze to the window, and I saw a car I recognized—a Nissan Versa that I'd signed a lease on only three months before—and any chance that it could just be a coincidence disappeared when the engine stopped, and the driver who stepped out had a face I knew by heart.

A face that had earnestly sworn to never take the car out on the highway if I wasn't with him when I'd handed over the keys.

And the only way to get here from Boston was by highway, so either he'd broken that promise—and he was not prone to breaking promises—or I was dreaming.

Definitely dreaming.

Because why would Tate even be here? He thought I was at a conference in New York. He didn't have any reason to think I'd be elsewhere, and even if he did, he couldn't suspect I'd be at my childhood home, and he certainly had no way of figuring out how to get here. He'd been only seven when we'd last been here together. He didn't know the name of this town, let alone the address, and that was why he couldn't be here.

Could not. There was no way. This was not how Cade was finding out about him.

But the cold of the air blowing through the open door was undeniably real, proof that this wasn't a dream, that I was standing on my father's porch, that I was watching my son have his very first conversation with the one other man who meant the most to me, and I was seriously about to have a panic attack.

"Jolie's your...*mom*?" Cade's expression had gone hard. He was good at shutting down his emotions from view, a skill he'd perfected when we'd lived together seventeen years ago to help him survive the monster who was my father.

The skill *I'd* perfected back then was freezing up, and I was frozen now, my chest tight and my head screaming to *do something*, my body unable to move.

"Um, yeah. I wasn't sure I was in the right place." He gave his best grin. "But I guess I am. I'm Tate, by the way."

It was just like my kid to befriend a stranger. He was always sweet and polite, and for the most part, unafraid. I'd done my best to give him a life that allowed him to trust that people were good. It was the life I'd longed for and so it was the one I'd wanted for him, and in any other situation, I'd have taken this as a win.

But now I saw how I'd done him a disservice because I loved Cade—I'd both fallen for him again, and I loved him still —but I could admit he wasn't ready for this, and rightly so, he might lash out. As much as I wanted to fight to preserve whatever had been repaired between us over this last week, I had to think of my son first.

With that thought in mind, I could finally move.

I took a step out, then drew back quickly when I remembered I was still barefoot, and the ground was covered with snow. "Tate, get in here," I snapped, ignoring the strong desire to ask what the hell he was doing here. That could wait. This, however, was immediate. "Now. Right now."

Confusion marring his brow, Tate took a step toward me, but Cade grabbed his arm, sending warning signals shivering down my spine. "Wait. How old are you, Tate?"

"Leave him alone, Cade." Keeping the front door ajar so I could hear what was happening, I opened the coat closet, remembering I'd seen Carla's house slippers in there when we'd hung up our coats the night before. "Tate, come on. Get in here."

I had one slipper on and was looking for the other, when instead of listening to me and coming in the house, my son answered. "Almost seventeen. You're...*Cade*?"

"Tate!" I hadn't used that sharp of a tone with him since he almost stepped into the road chasing after the cat when he was eight, but this conversation couldn't happen like this. Absolutely could not.

Fuck the other slipper, I was going out like this.

Except then Carla popped up behind me. "Ah! He's here!"

Hold up. She was *expecting* Tate?

I spun back toward her. "This was *you*?" I couldn't imagine how she'd done it, but if she was somehow behind my child being somewhere he absolutely should not be... Rage surged through me, curling my hand into a fist when I'd never hit anyone in my life.

"What month?" Cade asked, ignoring Tate's question.

Fuck. I didn't have time for Carla.

Turning away from whatever bullshit response she started to give me, I ran down the steps so fast I didn't even feel the cold on my one bare foot, reaching Tate just as he said, "What month is my birthday? January. January sixth."

It was easy enough math, and I saw Cade doing the calculations, saw him figuring it out or thinking he'd figured it out, and there was nothing I could do but stop it. "Tate, please." I pushed him toward the door. "Go inside."

His expression gave just as much away as Cade's. "But Mom—"

I cut him off. "Seriously, Tate. Go. In. The. House. I'll be there in a minute."

"Jesus, okay. Fine."

I cringed. His choice of language was pretty trivial in light of everything else, but motherly instinct wasn't always great at prioritizing, and I had to resist the urge to correct him.

With his duffel bag in hand, he brushed past me, and while I wanted to follow him up the stairs and apologize and explain, I had to say something to Cade first.

Cade. My love. My only.

Cade, whose eyes pierced me like nails, accusing and angry,

holding my gaze to his, demanding explanations that I couldn't give until my son was out of earshot.

"Come right on in, Tate. I'll get you some hot chocolate."

Goddammit. Carla.

I tore my eyes from Cade and swung my head around. "Don't fucking say a word to him until I'm in there."

She glared as Tate walked past her into the house. "I'm just warming the kid up, Julianna. No need to go all mother bear on me."

She hadn't seen mother bear. This was a kitten in comparison with what I felt inside, and her play-innocent gaslighting wasn't helping calm me. Acting as if I hadn't just sent my child into a house with a wolf when her teeth were practically bared. I almost left Cade to go deal with her instead.

"You didn't tell me? You weren't going to fucking tell me?"

Just like that, my focus was back on Cade. "You're wrong. It's not—"

He cut me off. "No, *you're* wrong. What you did is wrong. What you did—"

I raised my voice, trying to get a word in edgewise. "I didn't do what—"

"—is unforgivable. You *robbed* me—"

"He's not yours!" It came out as a shout, and immediately, I worried I'd been loud enough to carry inside. But the front door was still closed when I glanced behind me, and now I had Cade's attention, so I said it again at a more reasonable volume. "He's not yours."

It was a gut punch for me to say it, even now, after all these years.

It had to be just as bad to hear it.

"But his birthday...?" As hard as his mask was, I could see the hope flicker.

Or maybe it wasn't hope but the flame of resistance. The desire to see the past as he believed it to be, that belief so strong that it was easier to bend the facts to fit around that than consider he'd never known the truth.

The truth he now had to consider was probably earth-shattering.

And while the whole truth might make it better, it would take so much more explaining than what I could give to him standing outside, perched on one foot so the bare one didn't hit the cold ground while my son got interrogated by his step-grandmother in the house behind me.

The whole truth was hard enough under the best of circumstances. I still had a hard time saying it out loud.

"If he's going to be seventeen in January..." Cade wasn't going to give up so easily. "That means you got pregnant your senior year. Nine months. That means you were pregnant at graduation."

I wished I could lie, but all I could say was, "Right."

Then he understood. His shoulders slumped, his expression fell. I'd gotten pregnant while we were together, and the baby wasn't his, and that meant...

"Oh." He took a step backward. Then another. "I see."

But he didn't see, and while he now realized I hadn't robbed him of the chance to watch his child grow up, I wasn't sure that this new epiphany was any easier to forgive.

"Cade." It came out like a plea, even though I knew that wasn't fair.

He shook his head at me, confirming that I had no right to ask him anything now—maybe not ever again—and took another step backward, another step away from me. "I'm such an idiot."

"No." I stepped after him, reaching for him. "You're not."

"Such a fucking idiot."

"You aren't. I need to explain. I need to—"

But he wasn't hearing me. As though in a daze, his head still shaking, he turned toward our rental car. "I, uh, have to get to the locksmith."

He couldn't hide the hurt on his face, though he was trying. And as many times as I'd imagined telling him, his reaction was somehow way worse than any scenario I'd thought up on my own.

I'd broken him.

Again.

How many times could I do this to him and still hope that he could be put back together?

I felt the ache as though it were mine.

Whatever was happening inside the house, it was suddenly not as important as this. "Cade, wait. Please. Let's talk." I chased after him.

He was at the driver's side of the car. "I can't." He opened the door. "I have to..." Instead of finishing the sentence with words, he held up the keys to my father's cabin that we'd found while searching his office the night before, the keys he planned to take to town to get copied.

I didn't have my coat or my purse or a proper pair of shoes, but I ran to the passenger door. "I'll go with you." I pulled on the handle, but it was locked. I pulled again, as if that would magically make it open. "Please, let me come."

He paused, one foot in the car, refusing to look me in the

eye. "I'd really rather be alone right now." He nodded at the house. "You should go be with your *son*."

He threw the word like a dagger, and while I knew this was the worst way for him to find out and that he might understand if he heard all of it, I also felt validated. This was why I hadn't told him. This was why I'd kept this secret, even when I'd come back into his life.

Because the only thing he could do with this information was hate me.

Or I could tell him more, and he'd hate himself.

I honestly didn't know which was worse.

So I let him get in the car, and when he started the engine, I backed up and let him drive away.

THREE
JOLIE

Cade took a piece of my heart with him as he tore out of the driveway. But the other piece of my heart was inside the house, alone with a woman who could destroy what Tate believed the same way I'd just destroyed Cade.

My focus had to be on my son.

Back in the house, I didn't bother to kick off the slipper and instead went looking for Tate. I was already headed down the hallway toward the dining room when he called out. "Mom?"

I turned around and found him with his phone in hand, sitting on the couch in the living room, a space that was a complete contradiction to its name. Growing up, we'd only ever used the room for guests, and since I was very rarely allowed to have people over, I spent very little time there. I'd gotten so used to thinking of it as a useless room, I hadn't even bothered to look there, and now that I was looking, it felt odd to see Tate sitting there, being treated like a stranger in a house I knew so well.

It wasn't a bad thing.

In fact, I preferred it, but I was surprised that Carla wasn't beside him, telling him all sorts of things I didn't want him to know.

"Mom, what's going on? You're being so weird, and that man outside—"

I cut him off. "No, no, no. You don't get to ask questions until I get answers. What the—?" I paused to take a breath in and out before going on. However he got here, it wasn't on his own, and that meant I shouldn't be taking out my frustration on him. Slightly calmer, I asked, "What are you doing here?"

He looked at me like I'd grown two heads. "Are you messing with me?"

"No. I'm one hundred percent not messing with you. Why are you here?"

"You're scaring me right now, Mom."

Whether he deserved it or not, my rope was at its end. "Tate. Just answer the goddamn question."

"Why are you yelling at me? You told me to come!"

"I did not! When?"

With a huff of frustration, he clicked a few things on his phone and then stood up to show me. "Last night. Were you drunk or something?"

I read the last text he'd sent a little before ten. **Maps says I'll be there in an hour.**

The text before that from me had been sent a few minutes before. **When do you think you'll be here?**

Except I hadn't had my phone all morning, and I had definitely not sent that text.

A kettle whistle went off in the background. Carla fixing the cocoa.

Fucking Carla.

I snatched the phone out of his hand. Anger stirred through me, my body vibrating as I scrolled up through several texts until I found the last text I'd sent the night before at dinner, reminding him that he couldn't have anyone over and that I didn't want him driving after ten p.m.

I'd stormed off from the table, leaving my phone behind before he'd responded. **Tara and I are going to hang with Ben over at her place. I'll take the train back if we're out too late.**

If I'd seen that, I would have told him to be sure he didn't stay out too late.

Instead, the screen showed I'd responded around eight.
What are your plans for tomorrow?

Homework and cleaning my room. Duh. A winking emoji followed.

Why don't you drive up and join me instead? I stifled a growl.

In NY?

No, I'm in Connecticut now.

Wth r u doing in CT?

Change of plans. You should drive up. It's only a couple of hours away.

Tonight?

No.

There had been a pause before "I" added, **Tomorrow morning. First thing.**

He must have tried to call after that because his next message said, **Mom, answer!**

Can't talk right now. Let me know when you're

on your way in the morning. The address followed that as well as a link to directions on Maps.

Okey dokey.

The next text came from Tate as well, sent a little before nine this morning. **Still want me 2 come?**

Yes. Bring an overnight bag.

Should I tell the Burritts?

I'll call them later today.

Then I was back to the text asking when he'd arrive, and it took everything in me not to throw his phone at Carla's curio cabinet.

"What's going on, Mom? Am I in trouble? You're really freaking me out."

Another breath. I'd worked really hard to be sure that I always handled anger constructively in front of him, and I wasn't going to let Carla's meddling be the reason I ruined that now. "It's, um, no. You're not in trouble. I just... I didn't send these messages."

The color drained from his face. "What do you mean? They say they're from you. How can they not be from you?" He took the phone back from me and clicked on one of my texts, bringing up the contact info, verifying it had indeed been sent from my phone.

"It did come from my phone. I just wasn't the one..." He looked terrified and confused, and I hadn't seen him in a week, and suddenly, I really needed to hug him. "It's fine," I assured him as I wrapped my arms around him. "I'm glad you're here. I was just surprised, is all."

"I don't understand." He pulled away, much earlier than I would have liked, but I couldn't be too disappointed since he'd let me hug him longer than usual. "If you didn't send..." He seemed to have a thought. "When I turned onto the road and saw the school, I thought you were going to tell me you got a job here or something, but then I got to the house—this is where you grew up, isn't it?"

"I..." I wasn't prepared to talk about this. He'd been seven when we'd left—old enough to have memories of the place—but I'd hoped those were few and faint.

Of course, when he was standing in the very house, it was harder to expect he'd forget.

"Do you remember living here?" Carla came in carrying a tray with three mugs and a plate of cookies, as if she'd been waiting in the wings to enter at the right moment.

I wondered if the chocolate was hot enough to scald if I threw mine in her face.

"Vaguely," Tate said, looking around the room.

I didn't like this. Didn't like him coming back here. Didn't like him wondering about that time or our life here or anything before that. "Hey, kiddo, I need to talk to—"

But Carla spoke at the same time, and she was the one who got his attention. "Do you remember me?" She set the tray on the coffee table and stood up straight so he could get a good look at her.

"You're..." He squinted his eyes in her direction.

"Married to my father," I finished for him.

Again, Carla spoke over me. "Cade's mother."

"Cade?" Tate perked up immediately.

Just like I feared, she had opened a can of worms that I was not ready to deal with. The situation was too complicated, always had been, which was why I had never wanted him to come back here. Now all my secrets and lies were threatening to unravel, and I needed to take control of the situation, right the fuck now.

"Okay, Tate. How about you go upstairs and rest for a while. I need to talk to Carla real quick." *And maybe murder her a little bit while I'm at it.*

I tried to nudge him toward the stairs, but Carla took that moment to put her hand in her pocket and retrieve my cell. "Oh, Julianna. You left this downstairs last night."

Tate didn't budge. "Julianna?"

I grabbed my phone out of her hand, wishing I could yank her arm out of the socket with it. Stupid me for leaving it out of my sight. Stupid me for using Cade's birthday as my lockscreen pin. She was probably the only person in the world who could guess it. Stupid me for not changing it before I'd stepped foot in this fucked-up house.

"Hold on," Tate said, pointing his finger in Carla's direction. "You had my mom's phone?" He was too bright of a kid to miss anything. "So who was texting me last night?"

This time, I didn't let her say a word. "I'm going to find all of that out, okay? I'll fill you in after. You can get a little rest before you have to go back home. Upstairs. The room at the end of the hall."

"Don't forget your cocoa." Carla looked smug as she tried to hand him the mug.

He ignored the mug and spun toward me. "You're making me go back home already?"

Whoops. Not the thing to say at the moment. "We can talk about it in a bit. Go lie down."

"I'm not tired, Mom. I haven't even had lunch. And why can't I be here for this conversation? I'm obviously involved."

"Do you want me to make you a bite to eat?" As annoyed as

I was with Carla's innocent/sweet step-grandparent routine, I was grateful for this suggestion.

"Awesome idea." I took the mug out of her hand and put it in Tate's. "You can stay here and eat some cookies, and I'll help in the kitchen." I nodded for Carla to go ahead of me, but she only took one step before he stopped us.

"Wait a minute, Mom. Please."

I smiled at him impatiently. "What?"

"Just tell me one thing." He put the mug down on the tray, seeming disinterested in the drink. "That man—Cade? That's Cade Warren, right? And don't tell me it's not the same Cade like you did when I looked him up that one time because you can't say that's not him if he's here. That's too big of a coincidence."

I'd hoped he wouldn't recognize Cade in person. It had been a year since he'd gone looking online for the name he'd been hearing about for years, determined to find the man who I insisted had disappeared. Thank God the name wasn't that uncommon. He'd shown me face after face after face, and each time I'd said, "Not him."

Then he'd actually shown me Cade—my Cade—dressed in a suit, listed as a co-owner of a huge international marketing firm, and my stomach had turned over on itself while I'd repeated the same "Not him" response.

I'd been caught out, and my face must have shown it because Tate looked hurt. "Why didn't you want me to meet my father?"

I could feel Carla's glare at my back. Shame flooded through me, the kind of shame I hadn't felt in years. Shame for the lies. Shame for not being able to tell the truth now. "Oh, sweetie." I tried to hug him again, but this time, he pulled away.

"Don't treat me like I'm a kid. Does he not want to meet me? What is he even doing here? Is that why she brought me out here?"

I was a shit mother. This whole thing he'd walked into had to be even more confusing and fucked up to him than it was to me—and it was pretty fucked up to me—even though it wasn't my fault that he was here, it was my fault that he believed the things he believed.

And my fault for perpetuating the lies. "He doesn't know," I said softly before I'd completely committed to saying it.

"He doesn't know I'm his kid?"

Now that I'd started down this path, it was easier to keep running down it. "He doesn't know he has a kid at all. He left town before I knew I was pregnant, and then, like I told you, I didn't know what happened to him..."

"But then I found him on the internet—"

"You did. And I lied about who he was because, if I admitted it, you'd want me to reach out, and it's just..." I glanced back at Carla who now had the decency to look as pained by this conversation as I was. "It's just that it's complicated, honey. And that's not fair to you, and I'm sorry, but please, can I just have a few minutes to talk to Carla? Then I'll try to answer whatever questions I can." It wasn't just about laying into her any more about the mess she'd put me in, though it was that too. Now, I needed her to help me figure out how to get my fucking story straight.

And maybe a moment to cry without Tate seeing.

He cast his eyes down and flipped his phone around in one hand, over and over, something he often did absentmindedly while he thought things out. "Complicated because Carla is both married to Grandpa and also Cade's mother?"

Yep. Exactly because of that, kid.

Surprisingly, it was Carla who had the comforting words. "They were seniors in high school when they met, Tate. It wasn't like they were brother and sister, but yes. As you can imagine, it does make things complicated."

My eyes started watering, and I had to blink fast. "Look, you have every right to be mad at me, and I promise I'll straighten everything out soon, okay?"

"And you'll tell him the truth about me?"

That was easy to agree to since I already had outside in the driveway. It was Tate who I had to come clean with. "Let me talk to him first?"

Reluctantly, he nodded.

"Cool." This time, he let me give him a quick hug. "Now I'm going to go help Carla make us some grilled cheese, and then we can all sit and talk some more."

Of course, it was going to be hard for Carla to sit down with my fist shoved up her ass but no less than she deserved.

FOUR
JOLIE

Past

I TUCKED my feet underneath me, tossing the ice pack I'd had on my breasts to the ground. They were so engorged, every little movement hurt. The hospital nurse had been the one who recommended the icing, but they only stayed icy for about fifteen minutes—ten with the stove in the den going—and I really wasn't convinced it was helping anyway. Now my tits were just sore and cold.

The nurse had also said it would take a week or so to dry up. Considering it had only been a day since my milk had come in, the near future promised to be more of the same. I groaned thinking about it.

"It's not too late to change your mind about nursing," Carla said from the rocker in the corner.

I glanced over at her, my eyes resting on the baby in her

arms. My chest tightened whenever I looked at him, a pain that had nothing to do with my breasts, and I had to swallow before I could respond. "I'm still thinking about it."

"I don't know what there is to think about. It's healthiest for the baby and for you, to be truthful. Not to mention how much money we'll save. Formula is expensive."

Everything was expensive—formula, diapers, doctor visits. The bill I'd been shown before I checked out of the hospital said I would have owed eighteen thousand dollars without my father's insurance.

That had been one of the primary reasons I hadn't left with Cade.

The other reason was why I had initially decided against nursing. The same reason the baby had yet to be given a name. I was trying my best not to bond with him until the DNA results came back.

What happened after that was beyond my ability to consider. It was one sleepless hour at a time right now. I'd deal with *what next* when it became *what now*.

"Who has a full tummy, huh? Do you have a full tummy?"

It was weird to watch Carla cooing over anything. I'd never imagined her having any maternal instincts at all, not just because I'd never witnessed that side of her but also because of the stories I'd heard from Cade. Maybe she was only good with babies.

Or maybe she was only good with babies who weren't her own.

She'd been a great help with the feedings, at least. The less I held him, the better. Because every time he was in my arms, I'd stare at his full lips and his wrinkly eyes and try to see Cade in his features. More times than not, I'd find him.

And until I knew whether those glimpses were real or not, I had to stop looking.

Carla unswaddled the baby, put him over her shoulder, and rubbed his back in circles. "Come on now. Let it out." She kissed his head and then looked at me. "Cade used to take forever to burp too."

Apparently, she was looking for him in my baby too.

It would have made me hopeful if I thought she suspected the truth. But she took it for granted that he was Cade's son, and so of course that's what she saw.

And I wanted him to be Cade's so badly that of course that's what I saw too.

A door shut in the front of the house. I hadn't realized it was so late. Day and night had blended together in the five days since I'd given birth. I'd been surprised when I'd come down for breakfast only to find it was time for lunch. Now I was surprised that my father was already home from his first day of the new term.

"Shit." It was under her breath, but I still caught the curse. "I haven't started dinner."

"Julianna?" He sounded like he was calling up the stairs.

I didn't answer. Instead, I held my hands out toward Carla. "Give him to me." Not because she had to go cook but because my father would find me soon, and bonded with the baby or not, I knew it was my responsibility to protect him from the evils in the world.

The biggest evil I knew lived under the same roof.

She swaddled him back up and brought him over to me. "He still needs to burp," she said just as my name was called again. "Your father is not going to be happy if he has to go upstairs looking for you only to find you're not there."

I hadn't been trying to keep on his good side for months now. Pregnancy had seemed to place me off-limits, and for the first time in my life, he'd left me alone for weeks at a time.

But I wasn't pregnant anymore, and I wasn't stupid enough to think a baby in his life would make him any less sinister.

"In the den," I shouted before taking the baby from Carla.

It was an awkward exchange—it always was, it seemed. It was like I made myself forget how to hold him, or I wouldn't allow myself to let the instincts of mothering take over.

But every time, as soon as I had him in my arms, he settled magically into the curve of my elbow—like he'd always been there, like he was an extension of me—and this time was no different.

"Hi." I couldn't help smiling. The corners of my mouth rose all on their own.

His eyes got big, and he made an O shape with his lips, as if I was the most fascinating thing he'd ever seen.

That tightness returned to my torso, and it suddenly felt hard to breathe.

Outside the den, my father must have bumped into Carla. "You're not in the kitchen." The words were innocent enough, but his tone was clearly displeased.

"I thought I'd do something simple tonight. Sandwiches and soup since it's so cold out." She tried to sound light and breezy.

There was a silence that I guessed was being filled with one of his seething stares.

"'Only peasants eat sandwiches for dinner,'" I whispered to the baby, quoting one of my father's convictions. "Learn that now, and you'll be ahead of the game."

Except it wasn't going to matter. Whatever we found out

about his parentage, he wouldn't be subject to my father's cruel rules and specifications.

"I'll do a pasta with meat sauce then," Carla said.

"I'm presuming dinner will be late?"

"Not by too much. You'll see."

I'd wondered sometimes if Carla was subject to my father's wrath the way Cade and I had been, but if I believed she was, then I had to wonder if my mother had been too, and I didn't like thinking about that.

In instances like this, I was sure she was a victim as much as any of us. I could hear the nervousness in her tone. Could sense the subtext in my father's question about the lateness of the meal. There would be repercussions for this, it said.

God, what a nightmare this place was.

"You'll be okay, Tate. I promise."

"Tate?" My father had entered the room too quietly for me to hear. "Is that his name?"

I hugged the bundle closer to me, ignoring the pain of the pressure on my breasts. "Trying it out, is all."

"It's nice to see you holding him for once. It seems like he's been attached to Carla since he came home from the hospital."

These were the kinds of remarks he was famous for—seemingly innocuous but loaded. *You're causing my wife to be distracted*, was what he really meant for me to hear. *I'm not going to tolerate that for long.*

I hated him.

I hated him, I hated him, I hated him.

"She's been great. Thank you for letting her help."

He stared at me. I could feel his eyes as I stared just as hard at the baby in my arms. His stares were almost worse than his subtle threats. They were harder to translate. What did he want? Would I be in trouble if I didn't anticipate whatever it was?

"You're leaking," he said after a long stretch of silence.

I glanced at the wet spot on my T-shirt and missed the cardboard envelope he threw at me, barely missing the baby's face as he said, "Oh, and this came."

I'd given him my share of glares over the years, but usually behind his back since looking at him "wrong" could earn me a week of not being able to sit down. This glare, however, I delivered right to his face, feeling a surprisingly intense and ferocious need to protect.

But before I snapped at him about his aim—which was likely purposeful—I saw the return address on the envelope label. **ScienceLife Labs**.

"Are these the results?" My father had swabbed me, Carla, and the baby only a few hours after I delivered and took care of mailing them off for a paternity test. He'd said we'd get the results quickly, but this had been fast.

"I'd suspect so."

I hadn't even opened it, and my eyes were already tearing up. My heart was in my throat. I'd been waiting for this since I'd first seen the plus sign on that stupid pregnancy test. This moment would be the one that determined the rest of my life. The rest of this baby's life, too.

It was too much. Too fucking much.

"You're not going to open it?"

I was still staring at the label—the envelope in one hand, the baby in the other. He suddenly felt heavier than he'd been, and I wanted to put him down, wanted to put him in the portable bassinet and leave the room to read the results in private.

But I wouldn't leave him with my father.

"I could open it for you, if—"

I cut him off. "No. I'll do it." I ripped open the envelope—clumsily with the better part of one arm preoccupied—and pulled out the document from inside. It wasn't fancy but official looking. The ScienceLife logo sat in the top left corner. My name and address were typed below it. Then in the center of the next line, the words *Paternity Test* were in bold.

DNA MOUTH SWABS *were examined from the following individuals:*

HNDS1987655Mother
HNDS1987656Child
HNDS1987657Alleged Paternal Grandmother

A BUNCH of technical speak followed, then a chart comparing the alleles found in our samples. I turned to the next page and scanned past everything to the heading at the bottom.

BASED ON OUR ANALYSIS, *it is practically proven HNDS1987657, the Alleged Paternal Grandmother, is not related to the child, HNDS1987656.*

MY VISION CLOUDED. If there was more to read, I couldn't see it. The paper fell from my hands, and I bit my lip to keep from losing my shit. *He's not Cade's. He's not Cade's. Oh, God, he's not Cade's.*

I felt sick to my stomach. Bile filled the back of my throat, and it burned when I swallowed it down. The worst part was that I didn't even have the luxury to grieve. A decision had to be made. *What now* was here. And I was not at all prepared to figure that out.

I could sense my father's glee as he sat down in the armchair next to the couch. He didn't have to ask what the report had said. It had to be written all over my face, and this kind of disappointment was exactly the kind of thing the man got off on.

Fucking psycho sadist.

"Are you going to hunt him down and join him?" My father didn't speak Cade's name anymore, but it was obvious who he was talking about. "Saddle him with a child that isn't his? Will you tell him, or will you lie?"

It was an option, one I hadn't wanted to consider. I didn't think I could tell him the truth, not all of it anyway, but I wouldn't lie.

And why would he still want you?

If he still loved me, I couldn't expect him to love me enough to accept this kind of baggage. It wasn't fair to force him to make that choice.

"Or are you considering adoption?" My father was exceptionally skilled at getting inside my head. He loved that as much as he loved any other form of torture, and right now, it was very much torture to hear him lay out my options, including the downsides, with pointed accuracy. "Is that why you haven't named him yet?"

I hated how well he knew me. No matter how hard I tried to hide myself from him, he still figured out so much.

Could I really give this baby away? A baby who wasn't

Cade's but had been made from me and lived inside me and had been the only reason I'd had to push on for the better part of a year?

I brushed my finger against his tiny cheek. His skin was so soft, it felt unreal. And those eyes! The only other person who had ever looked at me that intensely was Cade. He looked at me like I belonged to him, and I did. I really did.

Because even if he wasn't Cade's baby, he was mine.

And that meant he was my responsibility. It was my job to do what was best for him, and what was best for him was giving him up.

A tear slid down my cheek. I'd told myself I could remain detached, but that was a big fat lie. I'd been attached to him from the second I'd found out about his existence inside of me.

Giving him up was going to hurt like hell.

But I would. For him. And then I'd go to Cade.

"You don't even know where that boy went off to," my father said, once again inside my thoughts. "How do you expect to find him? Are you expecting fate to bring you together? What a romantic notion. I've coddled you too much if that's what you're thinking."

Another tear fell. What if I never found Cade? What if I gave up my baby and never found him?

I pressed a kiss on his tiny forehead.

"You could always leave him here with us."

My head shot in his direction. "Never."

I knew I'd made a mistake the minute the word was out of my mouth. I'd walked right into his trap, and there was no way to get out of it because now he knew my price.

He smiled as though he'd already won, and honestly, he had. The rest was just going through the motions. "No judge in the county will deny me if I make the request to keep him."

I shook my head, trying to pretend he wasn't saying what he was saying.

"I'm a well-respected member of the community."

"I'm his mother."

"An unfit mother. If I say you are."

I'd fucked up. Fucked up so bad. I should have gone with Cade. We would have figured it out. Poor and uninsured people had babies every day. And I would never have gotten a paternity test. We could have gone forever not knowing.

But that wasn't what I'd done.

"Why would you do that?" I asked, already knowing the answer.

"For the baby, of course. I couldn't let a baby with Stark blood be raised by a stranger. Not when we could offer him the best life here."

It was all a bunch of lies. This was the worst life, and he didn't give a shit about a baby with his blood. He only cared about keeping me here. Keeping me under his thumb. Keeping me his.

I kissed my baby's head again. Pressed my cheek to his and rocked him back and forth. When I straightened up again, I lifted my chin defiantly. "You will *never* lay a hand on him. Do you understand?" I didn't have any power here, but I played it like I did. Because if he *did* hurt my child, I would find the power, whatever I had to do to get it, and he would regret it.

"Whatever you say."

"And I am his mother. He's mine, and I decide what's best for him."

He nodded, a smug smile on his lips. "Of course. Just like I decide what's best for you."

I squeezed my eyes tight against the onslaught of tears. They were still closed when I felt his lips on my temple. "Don't cry, princess. You're doing the right thing. I'll take care of you both."

It was fucked up how a part of me could still believe him when he said things like that. Fucked up that I *wanted* to believe him. Fucked up enough that I probably deserved whatever I got.

When I opened my eyes, he was collecting the dropped paternity results. I watched as he opened the door to the stove and threw it into the fire. A few minutes later, it was like the report had never existed.

No one knew what it had said but the two of us.

"What will we tell Carla?" She thought the baby was her grandson.

He shrugged. "Let her believe whatever she wants." That kept it easy, at least. He nodded to my shirt. "You should clean up before dinner. I'm going to go change myself."

Just like that, everything was settled.

Another wave of grief rolled through me. Another sob threatened, but I choked it back. This didn't have to be forever. It would just be for now. We'd get out of here eventually.

In the meantime, I had to be strong. For *him*. For Tate.

"I guess you have a name now." I swore he smiled, though the textbooks said he was too young, and it was probably just gas. "It's you and me, little guy. I will always try to do the best I can for you. I swear it on my life."

And ten minutes later, when dinner was announced, I did what was best for the both of us—I stayed in the den and taught my son how to nurse.

FIVE
CADE

Present

THE SOUND of a car honking let me know the light was green. I drove through the intersection, then pulled into the first parking lot I came to. I'd been driving around so aimlessly, I didn't know where I was or how much time had passed. I'd gone numb. Like I had when she'd first shown up back at Reach. Completely numb.

Now, with the car idling and the windows fogging up, emotion pushed at the edges of whatever box I kept it in, wanting to get out. Wanting me to feel. Wanting me to acknowledge.

I'd wanted to know, hadn't I? Whether she'd ever loved me. This proved that she didn't—at least not the way I'd loved her because I'd been faithful. There had been no one but her. There was *still* no one but her.

And for her there'd been...

I couldn't let myself go there. I'd already tortured myself over the years, wondering who had been in her bed. Who she'd given her lips and body to.

But the curiosity was always about the time after I'd left. I'd never believed there could be any reason to doubt her fidelity while we were together. We'd been devoted to each other, hadn't we? Even if it had happened right after I'd left, it would have been a betrayal. What had I missed?

My mind scanned through hundreds of memories, looking for a clue. Her in my arms. Her at my feet. Her on my lap.

I landed on a time in the shower, when she'd snuck in just as I was about to get out.

"Dad left early for school, and Carla has a doctor appointment," she'd said when I told her it was too risky. *"I need you. I'll be quick."*

He'd been mad at her the night before, and I hadn't dared sneak into her room. It was spring, close to the end, when even speaking to each other felt dangerous, and yet we couldn't bear to stay away. In the same breath I'd told her she should go, I lifted her up and braced her back against the tile wall. Her legs immediately curled around me, and I slid bare inside her.

"I love you," I'd said as I pounded into her. *"Only you. Only you. I belong only to you."*

"I love you, too."

Had she said she'd belonged to me too?

Had she ever?

I'd made promises to her over and over, always telling her there was no one else, but had she? What had she said exactly?

As hard as I tried, I couldn't remember.

My jaw tightened. It was seventeen fucking years ago. It

shouldn't matter. I should have moved on. It shouldn't hurt like it was fucking yesterday.

But God, it did. Like the knife had been lodged there this whole time, and now she was twisting it with all her strength.

I took a breath in and let it out. Curled my fingers around the steering wheel and tried the old trick of tracing the tattoos on my hands with my eyes, hoping it would calm me down. Get my head focused. Bring me back to my prison of numbness.

But I didn't even get through one time across both knuckles before my mind had wandered; not to her this time. The boy. The kid with her eyes and my height.

And when I'd seen him, when I'd realized he was hers and in the minute that followed when I thought that meant...what it *had* to mean...

That was maybe the best and worst minute of my life.

Everything I'd missed was front and center—most people don't meet their kid when he's already full-grown, and the birthdays and milestones that had gone on without me were unforgivable even before I'd had the chance to recognize them.

But I'd wanted him all the same.

Wanted him to be my kid. *Our* kid. Made out of our love.

I'd wanted that to be her secret, and then I would hate her for keeping him from me, but I would love her too, and I would love him enough to make up for everything else.

"He's not yours."

Fuck.

I punched my fist into the dashboard so hard I wondered for a moment if I'd sprained it. Even that pain wasn't enough to dull the ache of the other pain.

I shook my hand out and stared out the window. I'd pulled

into the parking lot of a CVS. There'd been a Blockbuster next to it when I'd been in high school. Now it was a Dollar Store.

Nothing stayed the same.

Nothing changed.

Her son was what she was going to tell me about when all this was through, I realized. The reason why she thought I wouldn't want to help her with her father. A natural supposition. It made the imbalance between us obvious. She had her own life, her own world—her own *family*—and I was just the fucking tool she knew she could use.

Or I was the jackass who couldn't separate one thing from another.

Fact: Her father was a monster.

Fact: He was selling kids, and he had to be stopped.

Whatever had happened between me and her, that much was true.

He was the true bad guy here. I hated him without her in the picture. His crimes against me had nothing to do with her. He needed to be destroyed.

And I had the literal keys to his demise resting in my pocket.

I pulled up the car's GPS and located the nearest locksmith, then put the car in gear. This was what I had to focus on. Bringing down that motherfucker. Making him pay.

Figuring out how to feel about Jolie was going to have to wait.

SIX
CADE

The locksmith held up the key ring I'd handed him, singling out a small gold one. "I can copy all of them except this one."

That was the key I needed most, of course. The words *do not duplicate* engraved on it made it pretty obvious that was the cabin's safe key.

I'd been expecting this. I'd lucked out when the person who'd come to the counter to help me was a man. Women, I'd learned over the years, were more likely to follow the rules. Some heavy flirting could maybe win one over if she already hated her job, but it didn't work as often as it did.

Men, on the other hand, were much easier to entice.

"I was hoping you might reconsider," I said, handing over a Benjamin that I'd previously pulled out of my wallet for this specific situation. "It's sort of an emergency situation."

He blinked at the hundred, and considering he looked fresh out of high school, I wouldn't have been surprised if it was the first time he'd seen that big of a bill or at least the first time he'd been given one for himself.

"Uh…" He glanced at the front of the hardware store, likely looking out for a boss before he took the money and pocketed it. "I think I could help you after all."

"Thanks. Appreciate it."

He took the keys and began working, duplicating the engraved key first, his eyes darting back and forth from the machine to the front counter. "Stark Academy," he said, a nervous twitch in his voice.

It took me a second to remember the key chain I'd given him had the school's logo on it.

Dumb move. I should have taken it off before handing them over and would have if I hadn't been so distracted.

"Yeah, my, um, kid goes there." It was a better answer than the truth, but I was cursing at myself for having brought attention to me at all.

Though the hundred-dollar bribe had probably already made me memorable.

But now I was thinking about having a kid old enough to go to Stark Academy, and wouldn't you know it, the kid in my head had green-blue eyes and dishwater-blond hair.

"Son or daughter?"

He's not yours.

I cleared my throat, and the image in my head dispelled. "Daughter."

"Nice."

I was about to excuse myself to smoke a cigarette rather than continue to engage in painful small talk, but before I could, he started up again. "Crazy what happened there, isn't it? With the missing girl. Did your daughter know her?"

"Missing girl?" I was all ears.

"You didn't hear about it? I thought they would have sent some sort of notice home to parents."

"My ex gets all the school notices. I get weekends." I faked a laugh, as if the kid could understand custody arrangements. He laughed too, pretending he could. "So what happened with the girl?"

"I don't know a lot about it. Only reason I heard anything about it was because my dad's a detective with the police, and he said another student had accused someone who worked at the school of being involved with her disappearance. But then he said that that student was caught with a bunch of drugs and wasn't really reliable, and the girl was most likely a runaway. So I guess it wasn't really that crazy of a situation after all."

No, it was a crazy situation all right. And right on brand for Stark.

"When did this happen?" I already had my cell out of my pocket. "Do you know her name?"

He shrugged. "A couple of weeks ago? Thanksgiving weekend, I think. I don't remember her name, but I bet your daughter would know."

"Yeah. Probably." I dialed the last number that had called me and put the phone up to my ear. "Mind if I step away to make a phone call?"

"Sure. It's going to take me a bit to get—"

Donovan answered before the kid finished his sentence. "What's up?"

I stepped away from the counter, heading down an empty store aisle. "Another kid went missing over Thanksgiving. A girl. Don't know her name."

I could hear the sound of typing. Donovan Googling the

information, I suspected. "Are you sure? I don't see anything about it when I search."

"Being labeled a runaway."

"Of course. How did you hear about it?"

I wasn't going to admit my slipup with the key chain. "Overheard someone talking about it at the hardware store. Here's the thing, though—apparently, there's another kid who came forth and accused someone who works at the school of foul play."

"Daddy Stark?"

"Possibly. The cops dismissed it because the kid who came forth was in possession of drugs."

"Sounds a little convenient."

"That's what I thought." A partner in the police might explain how Stark had gotten away with his dirty side hustle for so long. "But also, you don't understand how that man is revered around here. He doesn't need anyone doing him favors. People believe the best of him already, no matter what proof is brought against him."

Donovan considered. "This is good actually."

He was often several steps ahead of me, but I didn't see anything good about another missing kid, and I said as much.

"No, but it's recent, and that's good." Another creak of his chair, and he was typing again. "Getting that drive in his safe is only step one, you know. It isn't going to bring him down until it's discovered, and it's not going to be discovered until there's reason to look. A recently missing kid could be exactly the flag we need, especially if there's a witness, and we can establish a pattern. Didn't you say that Arnold kid who went missing when you were there happened over a long break?"

"Spring break." And this had happened over Thanksgiving.

"I'll go back and see if I can detect that sort of pattern with the other missing kids. Meanwhile, think you can talk to the witness?"

I rubbed my forehead with two fingers, trying to ease the ache. "I don't know the name of the missing girl or the student who said it was foul play or how I'd get access to speaking to him, but sure. Why the fuck not?"

He didn't seem to catch my sarcasm. "I know someone who should be able to hack into the police file. If I can get that info back fast, you can make a stop at the school and play private detective."

"He might not even still be enrolled after being caught with drugs."

"Kicking him out would give the student more reason to voice his accusation. Stark is smart. He'll be there."

"I don't know, D..." I trusted Donovan with my life, but I was wary. As far as I was concerned, Stark was guilty, but getting a charge to stick—real or not—wasn't easy, from my experience. And it definitely wasn't going to work if we could be accused of setting him up.

Donovan knew what I was thinking. "It's harder to prove child abuse, Cade. This shit he's involved with now isn't going to go away just because you're caught asking some questions."

Except I wasn't just asking some questions. I'd also searched Stark's home office, was copying his keys, and was planning on planting incriminating evidence in his safe.

But Donovan was right when he said this missing girl thing was good because following this lead would be a distraction.

And I definitely had shit I wanted to be distracted from. "Get me the info, and I'll do it. But it has to be today."

Stark was due home from the cabin tomorrow, and I

planned to be gone when he arrived. Then I'd head up to the cabin myself to put the flash drive in his safe, and while I didn't know yet what I'd do after that, I did know one thing for sure: no way in hell was I ever coming back here again.

SEVEN
CADE

I paused on the steps to the house to smoke a cigarette even though I wasn't really in the mood for it, needing a beat before I faced the situation I'd left. The drive back from the locksmith, I'd been focused on the conversation with Donovan and the next task on our Bring Down Stark agenda, but now that I was here, I was reminded of the rest.

It twisted me like someone had tightened a cord around my middle, making it hard to breathe. Which was another reason I shouldn't have lit the smoke, along with all the other reasons cigarettes were terrible, especially when just a few weeks ago I'd considered myself in excellent shape.

Didn't stop me from taking another puff. At this rate, I was going to have a habit that needed to be kicked when I got back to Tokyo.

Tokyo.

The place I'd considered home for the last handful of years

felt so far away. So *not* home. Where was home then? It sure wasn't the place I was standing now. It was stupid to think that it might be the woman inside, but my head kept going back to her.

Just like my heart.

Stupid fucking heart.

It was beating faster by the time my cigarette burned out, both from the nicotine and from the anticipation of what awaited me inside.

Focus on what I'd found out in town.

Everything else was just noise.

Not quite convinced, I dropped the butt to the ground, hardened my features, and forced myself through the front door, not worrying this time about knocking.

My heart rate didn't slow any when I got inside and saw the kid—Tate, she'd said—sprawled out on the rarely used living room couch, typing furiously into his phone. He didn't see me, too wrapped up in whatever conversation he was having, a big goofy grin on his face.

I took advantage of the moment and surveyed him. He had Jol's nose and her thin fingers. His forehead wasn't hers—it was broad and protruded slightly, more like mine. It was a common feature, but I couldn't help myself from wondering—could she have been wrong? How did she know he wasn't mine? Was she really sure?

I knew better than to question a woman about her body and her cycle, but now that I thought after learning that she'd never felt the same as I did about her, could I trust her? Maybe she'd lied. Maybe she didn't want him to be mine, and so she'd decided he wasn't.

Or was that just wishful thinking?

I was studying him harder now, looking for something else that I could lay claim to, but before I found anything, he noticed me and sat up abruptly. "Oh, shit. I mean...hi. I didn't hear you come in."

He tossed his phone to the coffee table as though he'd been caught doing something he shouldn't have been doing by someone who would know or care, which of course I was neither. Maybe he was just a nervous kid.

"Yeah, I..." I pointed at the door behind me. Stupidly. Like he wouldn't know that was where I'd come from.

Fuck, maybe I was nervous too.

It was just because he was a teenager, and I was rarely around them. No other reason. I couldn't think of the last time I'd dated a woman who had a kid. Actually, I'd never dated a woman who had a kid. For one thing, fucking probably wasn't the same as dating, and that's pretty much all I did.

For another thing, Jolie and I were definitely not dating.

I don't want this to end with you.

Had it really only been this morning that she'd said that? It felt like another life. A life I wasn't sure we could go back to.

A life that didn't have a scrawny blue-eyed teenager staring up at me like I was an idiot.

I shook my head free of my meandering thoughts. "Know where Jol—?" I made myself stop. Made myself say it. "Your mother is?"

"She's in the kitchen with your mom. We had lunch, and I would have helped clean up, but then she said they needed to talk. They were going to talk before lunch, except someone came with groceries, and by the time my mother and I had gotten them unloaded, Carla had food ready, so we ate, and now here we are."

He was babbling. Definitely a nervous kid.

He must have read my face because he blushed and lowered his head. "You didn't ask for all that. Sorry. She's in the kitchen." He wiped his palms on his jeans, and I wondered if they were as sweaty as mine.

"Okay. Cool." It was my cue to exit this awkward scene.

But I couldn't get my feet to move.

"You should probably take your boots off if you're going to sprawl out on the couch like you were," I said, as though he needed parenting. And what the fuck did I care about his feet on the furniture? After all the months I'd lived here making sure to follow Stark's rules to the letter, I kind of wanted to put my feet on the furniture too. "On second thought, forget I said that."

It was too late—he was already pulling the second one off. "Right, right. Sorry about that."

"No, really, kid. It's not my house. I honestly don't give a shit what you do to it."

"My mother would."

"Eh, I suspect she doesn't care much about this house either." I didn't know anything about Jolie's parenting style, but considering that she'd lived with the same strict rules for even longer than I did, and from the attitude she'd had so far in the day we'd been here, it seemed fair to presume she felt the same.

He frowned, thinking that over. "She really doesn't like it here, does she?"

Now I frowned. What had she told him about growing up? How did anyone explain to their kid that their grandfather was an abusive asshole? "Uh...no. She really doesn't."

"She told me some."

"Did she?"

"I mean, not a lot. Just that she and my grandpa don't get along."

Well, that was one way to put it, I supposed.

And since I knew I couldn't be as courteous when I discussed our childhood, I took that as another cue to leave.

He stood up abruptly. "She told me about you," he said hopefully, almost like he'd sensed I was about to leave, and he really wanted me to stay. "Cade, right?"

Curiosity, probably. How often did he meet someone from his mother's past who could spill some inside dirt? Not that there was anything I felt safe spilling.

Problem was, I was just as curious. "Really? What'd she say?"

"Oh, uh." He flustered again. "Well, that um... She said you used to be in love?" He said it like it was a question, not like he wasn't sure, but like he wasn't sure he should say it.

My mouth fell open. I'd hoped that I hadn't been relegated to "Uncle Cade," but no way had I expected that. Especially after finding out she'd been pregnant with someone else's kid. If she'd really loved me, how did that happen?

But why would she tell her son that she had? Why would she have mentioned me at all?

"She didn't tell me that your mother married her father?" Again, another question; this time he seemed uncertain. "I'm just working that out as of today."

Yeah. I would have left that part out too.

It was strange, though, hearing it put that simply. We'd been convinced we would never be able to tell people how we'd gotten together, but all these years later, it felt more like an anecdote to tell at parties.

How did you two meet again?

Funny story about that...

Still, it was probably a little bit of a shock for Tate. "Yeah, it's not quite a traditional romance, that's for sure." Wary I shouldn't say too much, I couldn't help but add a clarification. "You know, we weren't ever like brother and sister. I didn't even live here a year, and more than half of that time, Jol and I were..." I reminded myself that he'd said it first. "In love."

He grinned, like my repeating of the term validated his sharing. "She told me you broke up because your family kicked you out, which now I'm realizing that your family was her family. Is that why she hates her dad so much?"

"Yeah..." I scrunched up my face. "I think it's safe to say she didn't like him before that."

This conversation was a land mine waiting to happen. I needed to extricate myself from it ASA-fucking-P.

But when I took a step, he took one too. "I'm Tate, by the way." He rocked back and forth, as though deciding if he should shake my hand or something.

He kept his arm down in the end, so I walked over and held out mine. He shook it quickly. A kid inexperienced with many formal introductions. "Just Tate?"

His phone buzzed on the table. He ignored it. "Tate Jacob Warren."

I froze, his hand still in mine. I'd half expected he'd have my last name—she'd taken it as her own, after all. But she'd given him my middle name too.

What the fuck was this woman playing at?

"Wait." He dropped my hand, his eyes wide in horror. "Is

that weird? It's probably weird that I have your name. I shouldn't have said that. I'm sorry. Fuck. I mean, not...sorry for cursing."

I really wanted to hear what he'd been told about why he had my name, but I also had the inexplicable urge to make him feel better.

The latter won out. "Nah, she told me. It's a good name."

"Phew." His relief was like a firework in my chest. "I didn't know... Hey." His phone buzzed again, and this time, he glanced at it quickly. "Can you tell me what's going on? Like...why I'm here? Because my mom didn't know I was coming, and this whole week I thought my mom was in New York, but then I find out she's here, and she's with you, and she'd said she didn't know where you were..."

He trailed off. Really, what was there to say at the end of that?

And what was there to say in reply? "Honestly, I'm not sure I know myself."

"But could you tell me what you do know? How did you two hook up? Has she been in contact with you all along?"

"First time I heard from her since high school was about a month ago." This conversation felt increasingly unsafe, so when his phone buzzed again, I nodded to it. "You need to get that?"

"No, I mean..." He sighed as he bent to pick it up. His eyes scanned over the screen, and that same goofy grin appeared.

"A girl?" Except it wasn't polite to presume that these days. "A boy?"

His neck got red, the same way Jolie's did when she blushed, except his didn't reach his cheeks. "A girl."

"A girl...friend? Or a girlfriend?" I didn't know why I was asking or why I was talking to him at all. It was possible I was stalling. The longer I stood here talking to him, the longer I could avoid talking to *her*.

And I liked this nervous kid. He was friendlier than I'd been at his age. Less hard, and just like he seemed to like what he could learn about his mother from conversing with me, I liked what I was learning about her from him. It was evident she'd made sure his childhood had been easier than hers had been. He didn't *yes, sir* and keep his mouth shut and his eyes down the way she and I had been trained.

In some way, that felt like a victory.

"Friend," he said uncertainly. "Or both. I don't know." Now the blush moved up his neck. "I asked her to the winter dance next week, as friends. We're going with a group, so not really a date thing, or I didn't think it was really a date thing, but since I asked her, we started a private chat, and I don't know." He shrugged. "I just like talking to her."

"That's how it starts." I could remember that feeling with Jolie like it was yesterday. Remembered trying to keep her at a distance, trying to keep her off-limits, trying to ignore how good it felt just to have her look in my direction.

"Well, now I don't know if—when I take her home at the end—do I try to...?"

"Kiss her?" He might have been insinuating something else, but I was fairly sure it wasn't appropriate to be giving Jolie's kid advice on anything besides kissing.

It probably wasn't appropriate to be giving him any advice for a myriad of reasons, starting with how much I liked the way it felt for him to ask in the first place.

"Yeah, kiss her," he agreed, and when he looked up at me with his wide trusting eyes, I knew that was another reason I should be walking away.

Still, I stayed. "I think you have to feel her out that night."

"Was that what it was like with you and Mom?"

My breath moved uneasily through my lungs. Thinking about the first kiss with Jolie was a tornado all on its own. Telling her son about it, his ears perked like it meant something, was a whole other storm system.

And if I stayed standing here—if I kept opening up and sharing and *bonding*—I was going to start to want him.

I was going to want him as much as I wanted his mother and the family the two of them made together.

But he wasn't mine.

And unless Jol had lied, he would never be mine.

There was an ache in my side every time I thought of that—low and sharp, buried in between my ribs—and I had a feeling that even when I had time to get used to it, that ache would still live there. A hard, malignant mass that never went away.

"Where did you say your mother was again?" It was an abrupt change of subject. Rude, too, and I knew the answer, but I thought it was better than just walking away.

Though, if I'd walked away, I would have missed the disappointment in his eyes, and that was both unexpected and brutal.

"The kitchen." The kid had tenacity, it turned out, and optimistically added, "Maybe we could talk more later?"

All he was asking was for a conversation. Probably wanted to hear more about his mom when she was younger. I'd already been haunted by the past since she'd shown up in New York. Why not share some of that out loud? Take him along for the trip down memory lane. Bring Jolie along as well, if she wanted to. What could it hurt?

The answer was me.

It could hurt me.

"I'm not sure about that," I said. "I've got a lot on my plate right now." I started toward the kitchen before he could respond, refusing to look back.

This time, if he was disappointed, I made sure I didn't see.

EIGHT
JOLIE

As soon as the kitchen door swung shut behind me, I tore into Carla. "How dare you?"

The words had gathered in my chest and had been worming their way up my throat for the last hour. I'd been ready to talk to her somewhat calmly when I'd first offered to help her with lunch, only to be interrupted by the grocery delivery. Tate had jumped to help—because he was a good kid, not because he was frightened of what would happen if he didn't—and I'd been proud of that, but it had left confronting Carla until later.

By the time groceries had been put away, she'd had lunch ready. Sitting at the table, listening to Tate politely answer her questions about his life, should have given me an opportunity to compose myself and find the best way to approach my step-mother and her outrageous behavior.

It's not so bad, him being here, I'd told myself while he blushed when asked about the women in his life. He was the best part of my life. I always wanted to show him off, and Carla had helped so much in his early years. It could have been a tender reunion.

Except I couldn't forget Cade.

Couldn't forget that pain washing over his face, and sure, it was going to hurt him no matter when he found out about Tate— and I had definitely planned on telling him—but finding out the way he did, with no buffer, with no chance for me to explain...

No. It shouldn't have happened like that.

He shouldn't have had to hurt like *that*, and it was Carla's fault that he did.

And when I thought about how many times Carla had hurt him over his lifetime—how deeply and how unforgivably—my anger built.

Not to mention that her method of interfering was an egregious breach of privacy, which should have been the main reason I was angry at her, I realized when I thought about it. As recovered as I was from my childhood, I still found it hard to put *my* feelings first. I'd spent so many formative years only caring about my father's feelings that sometimes it was hard to even figure out what my feelings were.

But given the time during lunch to evaluate the situation, I'd definitely figured out that I was downright pissed.

"How fucking dare you," I repeated, low enough to not be heard by Tate in the other room but with enough fury woven through the words that there would be no mistaking how enraged I was.

With a roll of her eyes, she turned away from me and started on the dishes at the sink. "Oh, settle yourself down, Julianna. He got here in one piece. No harm, no foul."

I bristled at the name that I considered dead, even though I preferred that to having my real name poisoned on her tongue, but when she got to the *no harm, no foul*, my spikes were fully out.

I wondered if she'd learned how to gaslight from my father because this was a load of lies if I'd ever heard any, and I'd heard plenty. *Lots* of harm. *Lots* of foul.

"You had no right. *No right.*" I was so mad, I was shaking. The stack of plates I'd brought in from the table rattled quietly in my hands. "To log into *my* phone? And talk to *my* son? Pretending to be *me*? No fucking right."

Her back still to me, she shrugged. For the first time in my life, I wished I had the power to instill fear the way my father did. Or at least the power to draw attention.

Desperate for her to take me seriously, I took the top plate from my stack—the same china she'd insisted we use the night before, the set missing a piece from my tantrum all those years ago—and threw it across the room.

The dish shattering made a satisfying sound.

It also got me what I'd wanted—Carla's attention. She turned first toward the mess I made, then toward me, her expression mean. "Real grown up."

"No, no, you don't have any right to tell me how an adult should behave, just like you had no right to interfere with my child."

"*He* had a right to know," she said definitively before turning back to the dishes, and I didn't think for a moment that she was talking about anyone other than Cade.

"You did not get to decide that for me. That was *my* decision to make, on *my* timeline." I resisted the urge to tell her that

I'd already planned to tell him. I didn't need to defend myself to her. "It was none of your business."

"You made it my business the minute you showed up here again bringing Cade with you. You expect me to stand by while you string my son along? Keeping secrets from him that he deserves to know. He should have known back then."

"Oh, please." I slammed the rest of the plates down on the kitchen table and was admittedly disappointed when they all remained intact. "It's a little late to play the good mother routine."

"I don't have to explain myself—" She cut herself off and swung toward me, a bread knife in her hand that she pointed in my direction. "You know what? How dare *you!* How dare you keep Tate from me all these years! I helped you get away. You think I would have given away where you were? You should have kept in touch."

She looked down at the knife in her hand, surprised, as though she hadn't realized she'd been holding it. Calmer, she set it down on the counter, but her back was still straight and her voice still firm when she insisted, "I deserved to be part of my grandson's life."

A whole new onslaught of angry words gurgled inside of me, but they caught in the back of my throat.

So that was what this was about.

I could argue that the way she'd treated Cade was cause enough for termination of any rights to his offspring, but that was neither here nor there considering the truth. And while I really wanted to lay into her for decades' worth of hurts, I knew the most productive use of my energy was to simply set her straight. "He's not your grandson."

"Don't do that, Julianna. You can't cut me off from him just because—"

"He's not Cade's son," I clarified.

She frowned. "But you had a DNA test. And Tate...you just told him that—"

"I know what I said, and..." I sighed. "I lied."

"You lied to your son about who his father is." It was less a question and more of an accusation.

At least, that's how I heard it.

Which was about right because I felt pretty damn guilty about it.

Funny how I'd never regretted the lie before now. I'd never expected I'd be caught in it, and the story was much more tolerable than the truth.

I half sat/half leaned against the table. "The DNA test showed Tate had no relation to you. I didn't tell you because...well, honestly, it was easier. And you never asked. Maybe that's not fair because I knew what you believed, and I let you believe it because, like I said, it was easier."

She let the water keep running, but she turned around so her back was to the sink and leaned heavily against the counter. So heavily, I wasn't sure she'd still be standing if she didn't have it to keep her up.

As if I needed more guilt.

I hadn't realized it would matter so much to her. It wasn't like she'd ever acted like she cared about any one of us.

"Look, I'm really sorry." The words came out so naturally, especially being here in this house, and a beat had to pass before I took them back. "No, actually, I'm not sorry. I didn't realize it affected you, and maybe if I had I would have told you the truth, but I'm not sorry for letting you believe what you did because it made it easier for *me* to believe it, and I really needed to believe he was Cade's."

She was quiet.

I wasn't sure what I was waiting for her to say, but I let several seconds go by in case she felt the urge to fill them. "I think I actually convinced myself he was Cade's. So by the time Tate started asking about his father, I didn't even think before I told him. If I had thought, I would have probably chosen the same answer. I just..." I rolled my neck, trying to loosen the tension that was most definitely related to the headache that was suddenly pounding behind my eyes.

And I thought about my reasons.

And reminded myself I didn't owe Carla anything, but saying it out loud was helpful because I was trying to understand my reasons myself. "I just wanted my child to have all the love possible. I wanted him to feel wanted, even if he was unplanned. I wanted him to feel like he came from something beautiful because I know firsthand how ugly beginnings breed hatred and self-loathing. I didn't want him to ever feel ugly. He's the most beautiful part of me, even without the lie. You know?"

"I know." Her voice was soft, and I had a feeling she was thinking about how Cade was the most beautiful part of her too, and as much as I didn't like her, she got credit for recognizing that fact at least.

"And that's why I hadn't told Cade yet. Not because I was trying to keep his son from him but because I knew he'd hurt when he found out that I had a son who wasn't his."

Carla lifted her head, and I thought I saw a flicker of regret in her eyes. Then defiance. "But he has Cade's lips," she said.

I'd thought that before myself. "He has Channing Tatum's lips too. If you look hard enough."

"Who's Channing Tatum? His real father?"

I chuckled. "No. It doesn't matter."

The door swung open, and I stood abruptly and threw Carla a *shh*, expecting to see Tate on the other side.

But it was Cade who walked in, his large frame filling the room. He hadn't taken up so much space when we'd worked side by side in the kitchen all those years ago. He'd outgrown the space over the years, and now he looked incredibly displaced.

I wondered if I looked the same to him or if I looked like I was right where I belonged.

The thought made me sick.

Seeing him made me sick.

It made my chest warm, too, and I wanted to reach out and touch him so badly it hurt.

"Hey," he said, his eyes darting from me to his slumped mother to the broken plate on the floor. He didn't seem to find any of it unusual, and his eyes swept back to me. "Can we talk in private?"

"Yes!" It came out too eager. "Yes. Of course. I didn't hear you come in." I'd spent the whole time he was gone thinking about what I had wanted to say to Carla and didn't have anything prepared for him, but I was beyond relieved that he wanted to give me a chance to explain.

I hadn't let myself acknowledge the thought, but now that he was here, I realized how scared I'd been that he might not come back. He could have gotten in that car and kept on driving, and I wouldn't have blamed him at all.

He half shrugged, as though he didn't know what to say to that. "Got here about ten minutes ago."

I cringed inwardly, afraid of whatever conversation he might have had with Tate. It was Cade who had come looking for me and not my son, though, so if anything had been discussed, at least Tate wasn't upset by it.

It was only a partially soothing thought. Eventually, I had to talk to Tate about Cade, and I didn't imagine that conversation was going to go well at all.

One aggrieved man at a time.

"Should we go upstairs?" I offered. "Or I can get some shoes, and we can go on the porch?"

He looked down at my bare feet and back at the broken plate, and even though he didn't express any concern out loud, my chest felt warm.

"You can have the kitchen," Carla said, turning off the sink. "I'm not in the mood to deal with the dishes." Her gaze also drifted to the shattered dish before coming back to me. "The broom's where it's always been, Julianna."

"Yes, I'll clean it up."

She'd left the room before I'd finished speaking.

Cade looked questioningly after her, but he refrained from asking.

"I've managed to piss off both the Warrens today it seems," I said, trying to lighten the mood.

He didn't even hint at a smile.

"Listen, Cade—"

He cut me off. "Here are the original keys. You should get them back to where you found them as soon as possible, in case Carla goes looking and finds them missing."

I took the keys from his outstretched hand. "You got them copied?"

"I left the spare set in the glove box. I didn't want to chance leaving them here or having them discovered."

"Good thinking." I slipped the keys in my pocket and took a step toward him.

He stepped away, so casually I wasn't sure he'd meant to avoid me or not, especially when he reached for a glass from a cupboard and filled it with water. "Is the office still unlocked, or do you need me to pick it again?"

Carla and I had left my father's office at the same time the night before. "I think it's still unlocked."

"Let me know."

"Okay." I took another step toward him while he gulped back the water, and this time, I was certain he was keeping his distance when he once again stepped away. "Can we please talk about this?"

"Nothing to talk about."

"Don't say that. You know there's a lot to talk about, and I'm here and willing—"

He interrupted again. "You had the right idea when you said we should hold off having any serious conversations until this is over with. We need to keep focused."

I'd thought it was the best plan at the time, but that had been before Tate had shown up, and the way Cade kept moving away from me had me worried that if we didn't talk about it now, he'd be too far out of reach to talk about anything at all when this was over. "I think it might be better if I can just explain—"

"Another kid's gone missing, Jol."

"What?" If he'd meant to distract me, it worked.

He pulled his phone out and unlocked the screen, then handed it over to me. "This girl. A few weeks back. I heard about it in town, and Donovan emailed over what he could find. Apparently, there's someone at the school who made a report, but the cops aren't following up on it. D arranged for me to go over and conduct an interview. I only stopped by here first to make sure you got the keys put away."

He was obviously avoiding all talk of Tate—I didn't blame him—but as much as I wanted to demand that we have a conversation, another missing kid was certainly more pressing. "Let me finish getting dressed. I'll come with you."

"I can handle this on my own."

"I know you can, but you're not going to."

"There's no need for two of us—"

"Cade, we're doing this together. This isn't up for debate. Don't forget what happened the last time you tried to keep me out of a part of this plan."

His mouth tightened as he remembered when I'd followed him to meet up with Donovan's contact, and I tried not to see Tate in the shape of his lips. He was about to argue with me, but when I handed him back his phone, I let my fingers brush his, and even though he yanked his hand away, the touch softened him.

Not much, but enough. "Fine. I'm not going to waste time or energy arguing. Hurry and get dressed, and put back the keys, and I'll..." He looked once again at the broken plate. "Clean up your mess in the meantime, I guess."

Apparently, he didn't need any explanation to know it had been me who'd thrown it. I suspected he was only volunteering to take care of it so that he wouldn't have to deal with Carla or Tate while he waited.

Fair enough.

But before I could let it go... "I know you don't want to talk about this right now, but there's something I have to—"

"You don't have to say anything."

"No, it's not what you think. It's just..." God, this would have been easier if I could have told him everything else too. But we were on a time crunch, and this needed to be said now. "Tate thinks you're his father."

He stood up taller, drawing more away from me without physically taking a step. "And why would he think that?"

"Because that's what I told him. Not today. Before today."

His jaw went tight. I could see the muscles straining all the way down in his neck, and the space between us felt heavy and hard, like an invisible boulder had been lodged there. "You sure know how to keep the hits coming, don't you, Jolie?"

I deserved that.

I deserved worse than that.

"I'll tell him," I promised. "But not here. I can't—"

"I don't really care what you tell him, Jolie," he said sharply. "Not my kid, not my problem. Just don't expect me to play daddy anytime soon or ever." He shoved away from the sink and walked around me toward the door. "I'll be on the porch. If you're down in ten minutes, you can come with me. Carla can clean up the goddamned china herself."

I winced as the door banged shut behind him. Winced again as his words echoed in my head and tried to tell myself it was a good thing that for once he wasn't the one cleaning up my mess.

NINE
CADE

"You're sure he's not mine?" I hadn't meant to ask. I hadn't meant to talk to her at all, but there it was, out of my mouth the minute we stepped onto the sidewalk that led to the dorms.

With her eyes pinned to the horizon, she sighed, her breath coming out in the cold air in a cloud. "Yes. I'm sure."

"Why? Because of timing? Because he doesn't *not* look like me."

"I had a DNA test done."

It was strange how I could feel disappointed yet again. When had I even gotten my hopes up? And why?

And why was I letting myself think about it right now? "The dad can't be in the picture, though, if you told him he was mine."

She shook her head, her mouth opened as though she were about to say something, but I cut her off before she could start. "And you thought he *could* have been mine. Or you wouldn't have gotten tested."

And if he could have been mine, then why hadn't she told me back then? "Did you know you were pregnant when I came here that night?"

She stopped, her hands shoved in her pockets, and stared at me. "Do you want to talk about this? Because if you want to talk about it, then you have to really let me talk about it."

Of course, I wanted to talk about it.

And also, I didn't.

It was definitely not the best time to discuss it. I glanced at my watch. The afternoon was getting away from us, and we needed our heads elsewhere. It was a legitimate reason to put this conversation off.

Still, I couldn't help but be an ass about it. "I don't think I can hear anything you say right now."

"Then maybe we shouldn't talk at all."

There was a note of pain in her timbre that matched the hurt in her eyes, and I tried to feel satisfied about it. She *should* feel hurt. She should share this pain with me the same way I was sharing the pain from her father with her.

It wasn't the same, and deep inside, I knew it too well to feel anything but guilty.

We walked the remaining ten minutes to the dorms in silence, but my head was still wrapped up in the past.

Being on the school grounds didn't help. Even if I wasn't focused on everything that happened between me and her, there were a hundred other ghosts there to haunt me. There were a few new updates to our surroundings—the greenhouse had been expanded, and there was a new building with a sign that said computer and library services—but mostly it all looked the same.

The same dull winter-white landscape.

The same asphalt pathway.

The same girl at my side.

The same monstrous headmaster dictating my day.

It felt like putting on an old pair of polyester pajamas. The fit was familiar, which might have been nice, but they still made me itch. This particular itch could never be scratched away.

It was better when we reached the dorms. There were fewer memories in the long stretch of student apartments since, for the most part, Jolie and I hadn't been allowed to visit anyone in them. If we'd had class projects or study groups, Stark had insisted they be held in the student center or the library. I'd managed to sneak into Amelia's room a few times to fuck quickly before the RA came by, but I couldn't have said now what floor she'd lived on.

I didn't remember the dorm lobby either. It had changed beyond recognition, or perhaps I'd only ever gone in the building through a side door using Amelia's key because nothing about the space was familiar. It was small with only a single couch and a handful of chairs next to a water dispenser. It was empty except for a student behind a glass-enclosed desk at the far side of the room. She had textbooks spread out in front of her and headphones on, and when I knocked on the window, she jumped in surprise.

"Hey." She slid the headphones down to wrap around her neck and slid the glass open. "Need something?"

When it came down to it, Donovan's version of arranging a visit with the purported witness actually meant just providing me with a name as well as verification that he was indeed still at the school. "Yeah, we're here for Terrence Moore."

My eyes flicked to the sign taped up to the glass with visitation rules, and though we were well within visiting hours, I'd forgotten that only family members were allowed to meet with students. Stark sure did know how to run a prison. "I'm his cousin," I added before she asked.

The girl's forehead wrinkled as she studied me. "*You're* his cousin?"

Jolie jumped in to rescue me from my apparent mistake. "Cousin by marriage."

"Oh. I'll call his room." She shut the glass again before looking something up on the computer, and I was half afraid she was hitting some secret buzzer that notified the cops about an intruder.

I felt slightly better when she picked up the phone. She spoke loud enough for us to hear her side of the conversation. "Terrence? You have a visitor." She paused. "I don't know. He says he's your cousin. He's a white guy."

Fuck me.

Yeah, it hadn't been the best tactic, I admitted. I had planned to say I was a private detective, which may have gotten us past the student "guard" despite the "family only" rule, but I'd changed my mind spur of the moment when I'd seen the sign.

Frankly, I blamed this on Donovan. He could have gotten us more information or arranged a face-to-face that sounded more legit.

The student was nodding now while eyeing me suspiciously. Fearing this visit was over before it began, I managed to slide the glass window back open and pointed to the phone. "Can I talk to him a quick second?"

The student seemed unsure, which was nothing compared to the look Jolie was giving me, but she put him on speaker. "Hey, Terrence, it's me, Cade. I'm a cousin on your mother's side. We've never met, but I thought we could talk a few minutes since I'm passing through town."

The speech was for the girl so that she'd feel all right about buzzing us in. Now I had to pray Terrence was curious enough to give her the okay.

There was only a fraction of a pause. "Give me a few minutes, and I'll be down."

I gave a smug smile to the student who still didn't look convinced. "ID and sign in, please," she said, pointing to a clipboard hanging on the edge of the desk.

I handed over my license, and when I realized she was only giving a quick glance at the picture before handing it back, I scribbled down a fake name on the sheet. Hopefully, she wouldn't remember my real name if anyone asked later.

As soon as I was finished signing, a buzzer sounded, and a door to the side of the enclosed desk opened. "Parents' lounge is the first room on your right. Make sure you sign out again when you leave." She put her headphones back on and returned to her work, already done with us.

"Ladies first." I felt unreasonably self-righteous as I stepped aside for Jolie. Truth was I should have been more prepared. It wasn't like me. I was too distracted. Too invested. Too off my game.

She seemed to share my frustration. "Way to assume everyone's white," she scolded as she walked past.

"I'm working with what I have, okay?" I hissed back, trying to ignore the cherry-blossom scent trailing after her. Why had I let her tag along again? She was the cause of my distraction. If this wasn't Donovan's fault, then it was definitely hers.

The parents' lounge looked much like the lobby except with more furniture. It was also empty, which was natural at this time of year and this time of day. If any parent was actually in town, they would have picked up their student earlier and taken them somewhere or gone up to their room. No one actually used the lounge for visiting.

That would be good for privacy, considering the conversation we needed to have with Terrence.

It wasn't good, though, for the meantime while we waited for Terrence to show up because once again, I was trapped with Jolie and the past, and this time, after pacing the room several times didn't calm my brain, I couldn't keep my mouth shut. "Who was it? Birch?"

God, I was an asshat.

I couldn't help thinking about whoever had been with her. Wanted to put my thumbs in his eye sockets and press hard.

Confusion skidded across her face, then dissolved into sadness as soon as she understood the question. "It's insulting you'd ask that."

"It's insulting that I *have* to ask." I wasn't proud of myself for it. I'd seen her fool around with Birch willingly, so it seemed a reasonable enough guess, but I'd also seen him try to take advantage of her.

The possibility that she might not have participated willingly in the act that knocked her up sat at the periphery of my mind, but I couldn't let myself consider it. That was a pain I wasn't sure I could live with. I preferred the pain of being betrayed, and so I focused on *that* pain until the possibility of anything else disappeared entirely. "If not Birch, then who?"

She nibbled at her lip for several long seconds before responding. "Does it matter who?"

Honestly? No.

The only thing that mattered was that it wasn't me. There

wasn't a single name that she could give that would make that hurt any less.

It felt too vulnerable saying that, so I shrugged the question off and paced to the lounge door. I looked out into the hall and found it empty. "Where is this kid?"

"He'll come."

If he was there right now, maybe I could stop obsessing about her.

But he wasn't.

And wrong time, wrong place, but I was a jackass, and I really needed her to feel as bad as I did. I shut the door again. "Do you even know who it is? Were you fucking everyone?"

She leaned against the wall and rolled her eyes in a way that made me feel like I was the immature one. "That's not fair."

"I'm not really sure you have a right to talk about fair right now." Looking at her made me all twisted inside, so I looked away.

But not looking at her made me feel twisted up the other way, so I paced back over to her and looked her dead in the face. "It might not have been a real ring on your finger, but we were engaged."

As far as I was concerned, we were anyway. She'd said yes. We'd made love in celebration. Anyone else she was with, she'd been cheating.

She shifted, giving me her profile, but I still caught the glimmer of tears in her eyes. "It was a long time ago, Cade."

"It doesn't matter if it was a long time ago or yesterday. I'm finding out now, and I deserve a chance to process it."

"Which was why I was waiting to tell you until after all of

this other bullshit was done. So you could have the time and space that you needed."

"Because you were always planning on telling me eventually."

"Not always, no. But that changed. I would have told you."

I believed her.

Which made me a sucker.

And I didn't want to be a sucker, so I tried to play like I didn't believe her. "Sure, sure. You would have told me everything, just as soon as I gave you everything. Again."

I paced back toward the door but only made it halfway there before a torrent of emotion swept over me like a flash flood.

I spun back toward her, my finger pointed at her like a weapon. "You know, it was real for me. I was in fucking love."

Her breath shuddered through her, and as many times as I'd seen her cower in front of her father, I'd never seen her look so small.

I felt even smaller for condensing her to that, and before I could think what I was doing, I reached for her.

Then her eyes flew to a point behind me, and when I turned around, I saw that the boy I presumed was Terrence Moore had arrived. "Don't mean to interrupt whatever this is, but I'm guessing you're Cade?"

A minute ago, I'd been desperate for him to disrupt this conversation. Now that he was here, I wished Jolie and I were still alone.

But Terrence was why we were here.

I answered the obvious with the equally obvious. "I'm guessing you're Terrence."

He came closer, looking me over. "Before you try to sell it to me again, you and I both know you aren't my cousin."

His dark skin made any blood relation improbable, and I had a feeling he knew his family tree too well to try to convince him I was connected by marriage. "You're right, and I'm not going to try to sell it. I just needed to get past the desk. Thank you for being intrigued enough to meet me." I held out my hand, figuring a formal introduction might be a good idea at this point. "Like I said, I'm Cade."

He took it, his eyes darting to Jolie, then back at mine in an unspoken question.

As much as I preferred leaving her out of this, she was here. I debated introducing her with a fake name. "This is Jo," I said, compromising. "My, um...partner."

Sure. Partner worked.

Terrence's face lit up with excitement. "I knew it! You're here from the police, aren't you?"

Uh... "Yeah." Jolie shot me an unsure glance. "I mean, why do you think we're from the police?"

He dropped my hand and shoved it into the pocket of his hoodie with the other one. "Besides the fact that no one else ever visits me? Look, it's cool. I know the official word is that Cassie ran away, but I heard the detective at the precinct talking with the FBI agent about the down-low investigation going. Don't worry. I won't say anything. Mum's the word. So are you here undercover or what?"

Jolie and I exchanged a look.

I was definitely rolling with this. "Obviously, we can't confirm that." I gave him my best nudge, nudge, wink, wink. "But I'm also not going to deny."

"Got it, got it." He beamed, thrilled to be in on whatever it was he thought he was in on.

"You said there was an FBI agent at the precinct?" It wasn't where I should have started, but an investigation directed by the police was one thing. An investigation involving the FBI was a whole other ball game.

Unfortunately, it wasn't subtle enough, and suddenly Terrence looked less sure. "Don't you already know? Isn't that why you're here? Is this a test?"

Jolie rushed forward with an encouraging smile. "We need to be sure we didn't miss anything from your initial interview and to make sure there aren't any contradictions. I know this is a total pain, but we need you to pretend this is the first time you're meeting with us, and we're going to ask you questions as if we know nothing about what you've told us before."

"Oh, okay."

"And I'm sure I don't have to tell you this," Jolie continued, "but it's my job to say it—it's best if you don't tell anyone at all about this visit. Is that cool?"

Whether it was her experience working with students or just her natural charm, she had him reeled in. "Totally cool. I wouldn't want to do anything to jeopardize finding Cassie."

"Of course not. Thank you, Terrence. We appreciate it." She gestured to one of the seating areas. "Should we sit?"

A handful of seconds later, and we were seated around a small table, my phone in hand, ready to take notes. I hit record on my voice recorder too, discreetly, though I had a feeling the kid would have agreed to being taped if I'd asked. "I'm going to ask you to start at the very beginning, but before we dig in, let's just clear up what you overheard. You're sure it was an FBI agent that the detective was talking to?"

"Yeah. He introduced himself as Agent Jones. He wasn't there the first time—"

"You were interviewed twice?" Jolie interrupted.

"Yes, which is why I didn't believe them about Cassie running away in the first place because why would they need to talk to me twice? And why would they bring in the FBI?"

Exactly what I was thinking, Terrence.

Jolie was stuck thinking something else, it seemed. "They interviewed you two times without your parents there? That's not legal."

"I'm eighteen. Technically don't need them, and it's a good thing because my mother wouldn't have let me say anything if she *had* been there. She doesn't like to get 'involved.'"

He made quote marks with his fingers as he said the word *involved.*

I didn't give a fuck whether he'd been interviewed legally or illegally. I wanted to know more about what he'd seen and who was being investigated. If the FBI already had their eyes on Stark, that changed everything. "So Agent Jones told the police that there was an ongoing investigation?"

He got nervous, his eyes bouncing from mine to Jol's. "I don't want to get anyone in trouble. Detective Aquilla didn't know I was there, or I'm sure they wouldn't have said anything. They'd dismissed me, but I thought I'd left my phone, so I'd come back to the room, and then I realized my phone was in my coat pocket, and I should have turned around then, except I heard Agent Jones ask if he thought I was going to tip anyone off about the investigation, and Detective Aquilla said he was pretty sure he'd convinced me that Cassie had run away, and he wasn't worried." He ran a palm over his thigh. "I wasn't going to drop it before that, to be honest, because I know what I saw, and if I didn't think they were going to get them, I would have made my parents pull me out immediately. Or I would have run away myself, I guess, since I'm old enough, and my parents seem to think I made the whole thing up, and no way could I stay here if I didn't think Stark was going down. Plus, who would want to miss out on that? I'm hoping they arrest him on a school day. That would be epic."

The kid talked so quickly, it was hard to follow.

It probably didn't help that we were only pretending to be on the same page as he was.

Fortunately, Jol seemed to have kept up with him. "Just to clarify, you think Langdon Stark is the person responsible for Cassie's disappearance?"

"I know he is. I saw her get in that car." He was convicted now, his expression solemn. "But it's not just a *person* who took Cassie. Headmaster Stark wasn't alone. He wasn't the only one."

The hair on the back of my neck stood up, and my skin felt prickly. "Who was he with? Do you know?"

"Oh, yeah. I don't know her name, but I know who she is— the headmaster's wife."

TEN
JOLIE

Cade immediately called Donovan from the dorm lobby after we'd finished talking to Terrence, and by the time we started home, the sun was beginning to set.

"Donovan knows that Agent Jones guy because of course he does," Cade said, a cigarette in between his teeth as he searched his pockets for a lighter. "He's going to reach out and see if he can get some inside information about the investigation."

He lit up before thinking to offer one to me.

I shook my head.

"You're so good." He inhaled, and I pretended it was the cold giving me the chill and not the compliment. "How you can manage to be here and not pick up old habits beats the hell out of me."

"I guess there are other old habits I prefer." I said it before thinking how it might sound. He was definitely the habit I preferred, but I hadn't *picked him up* because I needed the crutch. Or that wasn't the only reason.

But amending the statement was impossible without returning to the conversation he'd started before Terrence had interrupted us. It was a conversation that needed to continue, but it wasn't the most pressing topic.

Besides, I wasn't sure either of us were in an emotional state to handle it. Particularly him, after learning what he had about Carla.

That was a conversation that needed to be had too. If he'd let me have it with him.

He looked at me after the habits comment for a beat. I could feel his eyes on my profile, and I wanted nothing more than to turn toward him and show him everything I held inside. I wished it was the right time. Wished he would let me mean the things I felt.

I was strong, though, counting the steps in my head before I felt his gaze fall off me to the sidewalk in front of us.

The silence that had accompanied us earlier on our walk was too heavy to carry this time. Too many words needed said, and since he didn't seem to be interested in saying them, it fell to me. "If there's already an investigation on my father at the federal level..."

I wasn't quite sure what the question was pressing to be asked.

Fortunately, Cade did. "Then do we still plant the files we were planning to plant?"

"Yeah."

"That's the question, isn't it?" He inhaled and exhaled. "The FBI might already have copies of what's on that drive."

"That doesn't really put us in a different position than

before." It was possible my father already had copies of the "receipts" we'd obtained for the sale of children—God, it made me sick to even think about it—hidden away somewhere amongst his things. They'd most likely been written for him in the first place. The problem was that we didn't know for sure, and making sure the damning evidence was in his possession had felt critical.

Still felt critical.

"But if there's a chance that planting evidence interferes with their investigation..." He didn't have to say more.

"That seems more of a risk now than before, doesn't it?"

This time, when he turned to look at me, I was already looking at him, and he quickly flicked his eyes away. "We should wait to find out what Donovan learns before making a decision about what to do next."

"Will he really be able to discover anything more? FBI agents don't just go spilling information, even to their friends."

Cade chuckled. "They might if their friend is Donovan."

Good point. With only a few brief interactions with the man, I had a feeling Donovan was good at ferreting out everyone's secrets. He'd wiggled some of mine loose, and given more time, I was pretty sure he would have learned more.

Briefly, I wondered what secrets Cade had shared with him.

The prick of jealousy was unreasonable. I didn't deserve to know more of him, not without letting him know more of me, and still a part of me felt that I had a right to every part of him.

He certainly owned every part of me.

I resisted the urge to tug on his jacket and make him face me while I gave him all the parts I'd kept hidden.

Not now. Not yet.

"We'll wait then." I bit my lip to keep from saying more.

He took another drag from his smoke before tossing it into the next garbage can we passed along the path. "He's smart. Real smart."

"Donovan?"

"Well, I'd never say it out loud," he admitted. "But I was talking about Stark."

I liked it when he referred to him as *Stark* instead of *your father*. It was one of the reasons I'd changed my name in the first place. It let me disconnect from the monster. Let me be his victim instead of his daughter.

As for his intelligence, I wasn't about to be so kind. "He's not smart. He just bullies anyone who challenges him, and so people assume he's smart."

"There's truth to that for sure. But he's been clever about the way he's gone about this. I'd wondered how it had been so easy for everyone to write these kids off as runaways. Didn't they have belongings they'd left behind? Didn't they have friends?"

That had been one of the most useful things we'd learned from Terrence—Stark's method. At least the method in which he'd reeled in Cassie. He'd chosen a girl who'd kept to herself, which had to be purposeful. A girl who had been known for ditching class and wishing herself elsewhere. A girl who very might well have run away eventually.

Then, according to Terrence, he'd offered her something she couldn't resist: a chance to escape.

He'd sworn her to secrecy, of course. I was familiar with the ways he managed to be sure a girl wouldn't talk. Whether he was smart or not, he was particularly good at manipulation. The only reason she'd told Terrence was because she'd bumped into him outside after curfew, smoking a joint, when she was sneaking out with her packed suitcase.

She must have been too excited at that point to keep it in. She'd told him that Stark had gotten her an audition with a modeling agent in New York City, saying they'd let him bring one girl only, and that he'd selected her.

Terrence had promised not to tell anyone and bid her farewell, then watched her from the shadows when Stark's car pulled up. The cab light had gone on when she'd opened the door, and he'd seen Carla behind the wheel.

"If it had just been Stark, she might not have agreed to go," I said. The girls in my classes were smart enough not to trust an older man by himself, no matter what position he held in their lives.

But a married couple? That was harmless.

"Maybe not." Cade's voice was tight, and I suddenly felt like an idiot. It wasn't that I'd forgotten that Carla's involvement might be a shock to him—it had been to me—or that he might have feelings about it. There were just so many elephants in between us, it was hard to navigate without hitting at least one.

I fretted for a few steps, wondering if I should say something more about it. If he needed to talk, I wanted to be the one he talked to.

Honestly, I was the perfect person for him to talk to. Not just because I felt so much for him, but because I knew what it was like to realize you shared DNA with someone capable of evil. It was kind of a refreshing change to not feel alone in that regard.

Though, to be fair, maybe I was jumping to conclusions. "She might not know, Cade. He could have lied to her too."

He didn't ask who I was talking about. "We both know it's more complicated than that." He pulled out another cigarette from his pack and lit it.

It was complicated, and it wasn't. Maybe Carla hadn't known what she was part of, but she'd still driven the car. And maybe she hadn't known what he'd done to us, but she'd still let it happen. Maybe she hadn't known the truth about her husband's evils, but she'd been willfully ignorant.

No matter what grace anyone tried to give her, she was still guilty.

Yeah, I understood how that could be hard to talk about.

I turned the focus, instead, to myself. "I thought I'd made peace with everything my father had done years ago." As much as I hated acknowledging our relation, sometimes it had to be faced. That was something I'd learned about healing over the years. It's important to realize the past doesn't have to define you, but burying and forgetting wasn't really moving on. "I mean, it was over and done with. What was the point of holding on to it? I had Tate, and I needed to be in the present for him, and I couldn't do that with this huge weight dragging me down."

Cade looked at me intensely, not backing away this time when I met his eyes. "You just forgave him?"

"No," I scoffed. "No, no, no. Never." I reached out and swiped the cigarette from his hand, bringing it to my lips.

I broke into a coughing fit mid-inhale. "Fuck, how do you smoke these?" I asked when I could breathe again.

"If you don't like it, don't smoke it." He tried to take it back, but I moved it to my other hand, out of his reach.

Then I took another drag. Smaller. More manageable. "I like punishing myself."

"I'd tell you not to do that except pot, meet kettle."

"Oh, I know." I passed the cigarette back. "Anyway, not forgive, but forget. Or I didn't feel like I needed to confront him about it. I still don't. Not really."

"You don't?"

I shrugged. I'd imagined it for a long time—telling him off. Unloading and unleashing every stored pain. Preferably while inflicting pain on him. "I suppose I don't think he deserves the recognition. He'd enjoy it too much."

Maybe he wouldn't enjoy the hurting part, but despite everything, I was pretty much a pacifist. Any inkling toward violence made me feel too much like him.

"Yeah. He probably would." He passed the cigarette, and I took it, my skin sparking when my knuckle brushed his. "You said you *thought* you'd made peace. Does that mean you really didn't?"

"Obviously, not now. Not when I discover he's doing this. To other people? It was one thing when it was just me."

"And me," he reminded me. As if I needed reminding.

"And you." I inhaled. "But you were gone. So it was just me again."

"It was still bad when it was just you, Jolie."

I exhaled, pretending it was the smoke making my eyes prick. "Yeah. It was. I didn't always realize that."

It was sad how I'd minimized my father's behavior for so long. As if I didn't count. As if I didn't deserve to be treated humanely and without cruelty.

If I thought about that too hard, I'd break down, and we were too close to the house for that. I didn't need Tate—or Carla, for that matter—seeing me lose my shit.

"Anyway, again." I regrouped. Brought us back on topic

because I knew what it was I was trying to tell him now. "I'd thought I was past it. Thought I could live with him, and it would be okay. He was awful, but not always. Sometimes he was not awful at all. And he was my father. He'd been all I had for most of my life, and I'm—this is embarrassing to admit—I, um, I think I really believed it was love. How he treated me. I hadn't really had a whole lot of experience otherwise."

He opened his mouth to interject, but I didn't let him. "Until you. You were so different and so incredible. So unreal. It often felt like there was no way it could last, and I sort of kept waiting for the other shoe to drop. Which is partly how I was able to let you leave. It was going to end anyway."

Again, he opened his mouth, and I wanted to hear him say what I knew he was going to say—that he wouldn't have let it end. That he'd loved me. That it would have been forever.

It didn't matter if I believed it. I would have liked hearing it. Even now.

Especially now.

But that would have been said for me, and I was determined that this be for him. After he kept giving and giving, I needed to be able to give him something too, small as it was.

So I beat him to it. "It's not the point, Cade. The point is that I thought I'd made my peace, and it was fine as long as it was only me—"

"It wasn't fine," he muttered.

"—and then it wasn't only me." I let that hang in the air, letting him figure it out on his own. It was too hard to say it out loud. The guilt from this was the one guilt worse than hurting Cade.

"Tate," he guessed. We were at the bottom of the porch steps now, and he stopped and turned to me. "He hurt Tate."

I swallowed, afraid to talk.

Then I grabbed the cigarette from him, needing the buzz to distract me from the overwhelm of emotion. "He was, um, six." My hand trembled as I brought the stick up to my lips. "He'd sworn to me—" I shook my head, realizing I hadn't been clear with my pronoun. "My father had sworn to me that he wouldn't touch him. And I believed him. Because I was gullible and stupid, and I don't know, because I wanted so badly to believe that this human—this tiny miracle of a person—had changed his life as much as he'd changed mine."

Another drag. I was feeling nauseated, unaccustomed to the nicotine, but it was a much-needed crutch, and I understood one thousand percent why Cade was constantly sucking on one since we'd arrived. "I don't know how many times it happened. Or how bad it was. He'd made Tate promise not to tell. Scared him into secrecy saying I'd go away if I knew."

I shuddered, as I always did, when I thought about the psychological damage that had potentially been done to my son. He was as well-adjusted a teenager as I'd ever seen, and I still worried about it.

Cade's expression softened. "You don't have to—"

"Let me finish," I insisted. This was the hard part because it came with admitting my failure as a parent, but while it was something that I had fully intended on eventually telling Cade, it was the part after this—the easier part—that I was trying to get to. "It was purely an accident that I figured it out at all. Tate was practically never out of my sight. Or when he was, he was also out of my father's sight because I worked shorter days at the school than he did. So I didn't think it was even possible, and if I hadn't been paying attention, I would have missed it altogether."

"Jolie, it's not your fault." He took a step toward me, and as much as I was aching to be in his arms, I knew I couldn't touch him and not fall apart, so I stepped backward, putting my hands up to stop him.

"He was playing with his dolls—he loved playing house— and I happened to overhear him. Something the father doll said to the baby doll." I couldn't remember it now, but when I'd heard it, the hairs on the back of my neck had stood up straight, and I'd known. I'd just *known* because there was no way that he could know about discipline like that. "So I'd asked him about it, and he tried to deny it." I pointed the cigarette toward the house as a substitute for my father. "Because that fucking asshole knows how to keep a kid's mouth shut, but then he admitted it, and I realized what I should have always known— my father would never change. He was incapable of it. He *is* incapable of it. He was always going to get worse and worse and worse. It was never going to be fine."

I swallowed past the lump in my throat and hugged my arms around myself, careful not to burn my clothes with the cigarette, not ready to put it out.

Cade seemed to understand my need to say this now, and he waited patiently instead of trying to fill the silence.

It took several seconds. "I didn't have anything. No money. No education. Nothing but Tate, and I knew we had to disappear, or he'd find us. Which," I let out a gruff laugh, "might have been an unfounded fear. He told me time and again that he'd come after me, but that could have been fearmongering and manipulation. Who knows?"

"You had to believe it could be true."

"Yeah. I did. I knew I couldn't get anywhere without help. I really wished for you then. I can't even tell you—"

Deep breath in. Then out. "I broke down and asked Carla. Told her the truth. Expected her to brush it off, but she didn't, Cade. She got me the money and helped us leave, and you know that couldn't have been easy. Not the way Dad is. You know she paid for it somehow, and *that's* the point of me telling you this. It's too little, too late for you, I'm sure, but for me and Tate? She changed the course of our lives for the better."

I was the one who stepped toward him now. "And whatever things she knew about or did—whatever she's guilty of—she also saved us. So when you're hating yourself for coming from a woman who could stay in an evil relationship—because I know you, Cade Warren, you will try to hate yourself for it—just remember you also come from a woman who would risk herself for us."

Maybe it was even partly why he was so good at rescuing me.

This time, when he reached for me, I didn't stop him. He put his hands on my waist and bent his forehead to mine, not quite an embrace. My arms were still folded across my chest between us, but his touch anchored, and his skin was warm. "I'm so sorry, Jolie."

"Goddammit, Cade. I'm trying to give you something here." But there wasn't any energy behind my words. I *wanted* to give, but maybe I really needed to take too.

"And I'm taking it. Thank you for telling me."

"That wasn't what—"

"I know, but it was what I appreciated most." He lifted his chin so that he could skim his lips across my skin, then returned to leaning his forehead against mine.

"Okay," I said. "Okay." Because if I said anything else I'd

cry and because I'd give whatever he let me. "It should have been you she saved."

"It should have been both of us."

I didn't know how much time passed with us like that. I was so intensely present, so completely absorbed in the moment, that it felt like hours. But the cigarette still had its cherry when the door banged open, and we jumped apart like two teens caught making out.

"Tate!" I sounded guilty.

Seeing him, it was a whole new guilt that rippled through me. The guilt of lying to him about his father and the guilt of whatever he might assume having found me in Cade's arms.

"Mom, you're smoking?" he asked, eying the cigarette in my hand.

Fuck. Another guilt added to the mix. "No! I was just..." I blinked, no excuse coming.

"Holding it for me," Cade finished.

But I didn't want to feed Tate more lies. "I *used* to smoke. I was reminding myself how awful they are."

"They're fucking terrible," Cade said, taking the cigarette from my hand. He dropped it on the ground and crushed it with his boot. "Nasty habit to break. Don't ever start."

"Yeah. Don't ever start," I agreed.

"You used to smoke?" Tate asked.

I put my hands to my face and groaned. "Isn't it dinnertime yet?"

Tate shrugged. "Carla said something about having a headache, and we could fend for ourselves."

Good. I had not been looking forward to another meal with her.

Honestly, I didn't want to go back in her house at all.

Cade's expression said he felt the same way. "Hey, what do you guys say to bowling and pizza?"

It was a dangerous offer. One I shouldn't accept. Tate was instantly excited—too excited—and every minute he spent with Cade without knowing the truth would make it harder to come clean later on.

But I was fragile and only human. So I said yes and let Cade rescue me once again.

ELEVEN
CADE

Watching Jolie shoot little green men on an arcade screen was the first thing that had made me laugh in days.

"Why aren't I getting any points?" She shook the plastic gun, as if there might be a "bullet" stuck inside, even though it worked with a digital sensor. "Is it broken? I think mine might be broken."

Beside her, Tate was racking up the points, eliminating aliens with the skill of a pro. He gave her a side glance, so quick it didn't mess up his current hit streak, and shook his head in a way that clearly meant *God, Mom, you're so not cool right now.*

She glared at his profile, then tried pointing the gun at the screen again, her aim nowhere near any of the targets. "It's seriously not working." This time she turned to me. "Are you laughing at me?"

I stifled the laugh but couldn't rid myself of the smile. "Maybe this isn't your game. We should have stuck to bowling."

She'd been a shark in our earlier match, pretending she was

only a fair player in the first round until Tate accused her of holding back on purpose. The next two games, she slaughtered us both.

Since we'd finished our pizza by the time she was officially crowned the victor, we'd abandoned our lane and wandered over to the arcade section of the entertainment center, and while Jolie had held her own on most of the games we'd played so far, her skill apparently didn't extend to shooting.

"There was no way we could have bowled more. I couldn't handle how embarrassing it was for the two of you."

I gave her my best *fuck you* face, which I suspected looked more like adoration than wrath and only prompted her to give me a sassy smile in return.

Tate paused as the scene changed to nudge her. "Mom! The game?"

Even if she suddenly became an expert shot, there was no way she was catching up with his lead. Still, it was probably less fun to win if she didn't even try.

"Yeah, let's talk about embarrassing," I said, stepping toward her. "Let me help you."

I considered coaching from the side for all of two seconds before I threw that out the window, stepped behind her, and wrapped my arms around her. She stiffened in surprise, her breath hitching, then relaxed into me as I clasped my hands around hers and the gun.

Fuck, she smelled good.

Felt good too. Warm and soft, and I hated myself for grabbing the excuse to touch her like this. I'd tried to be careful all night, steering away from any sort of intimate connection, not just because I was concerned about giving her son the wrong idea about us, but also because I didn't want her to think she and I were suddenly fine.

We weren't fine.

And it wasn't like we'd been exactly fine before the whole *I have a secret kid* thing, but we'd been close enough that I'd thought being fine with her might eventually be possible.

After Tate showed up, I wasn't so sure we could ever be fine.

But for the past two hours, it had been hard to remember that. The activities we'd engaged in had required being in the moment, and as the present became more pronounced than the past, I felt...better.

Better than I had in a long time.

My body didn't hold its usual tension. My head didn't feel on the verge of a migraine. My stomach didn't feel like it was trying to digest a twenty-pound medicine ball, and air moved in and out of my lungs easier than it had in years.

So when I put my arms around her, it was only a little bit because I thought it was the best way to help her shoot. Mostly, it was because I wanted them there. Wanted to feel her heat and smell her hair and be fine with her.

"You don't get any points by just shooting everywhere and hoping you hit something," I said, my mouth near her ear. "Better to take your time, line up the shot..." I directed her arms so that she was aiming at one of the aliens. "And...shoot."

She turned her head to look at me, her lips so close I could kiss her if I wasn't focused on the shot and very aware of her son at my side.

I gestured toward the screen, needing her attention somewhere other than my mouth.

Slowly, she turned her head. "Ah!" she squealed. "I hit one! I hit one!"

"Amazing work, Mom," Tate said flatly. The Game Over words flashed onto the screen. "Maybe you can hit two next time."

"Oh, no. I'm not playing again." She escaped from my arms, and instead of putting the gun back in the holster, she handed it to me before walking out of range.

Tate looked more interested than he had a minute before. "What do you say?"

I paused, gun in hand. He wasn't my kid.

He wasn't my kid, and he thought he was, and that made this entire outing the worst fucking idea ever. Not just because he might develop some sort of attachment but because...

Nah. I couldn't go there. Couldn't think about it even a little. "Is it time to get some dessert? I think I saw an ice cream counter up by the bar."

"You scared I'm going to whip your ass?" He wasn't just taunting me for taunting's sake. He really believed he would.

Which made it much harder to walk away.

"Swipe the card," I said, taking the gun. "It's on."

Tate easily won the first round, but I held my own enough for him to prod me into another, and the second time, I'd gotten used to the game and edged out ahead at the last minute. So of course we had to play a tiebreaker.

Jolie cheered for both of us, praising Tate one minute and me the next. After her son performed a particularly good shooting streak, she frowned. "Should I be worried about how good you are with that gun?"

He rolled his eyes. "Because I might turn into one of those angry white boys who shoot up a school? Not the same, Mom."

"But if you—"

I cut her off. "Not the same, Jol."

And it wasn't. Not at all. I'd held a gun in my hand a hundred times. Aimed it plenty. Shot one off a few times, too, though never to kill. The weight of the real thing made it impossible to forget it wasn't a game, and the trigger required intentional pressure.

It didn't mean I didn't think Tate was capable of terrible things—anyone could be when put in the right situation—but I definitely didn't believe a source of entertainment was a predictor of such actions.

I mean, I was killing it in the game, and I wasn't running to gun down Stark. And I even had plenty of fucking good reason.

Tate grinned, obviously appreciative that I backed him up, and before I could stop myself, I grinned back.

"Good game," I said afterward, extending my hand toward him. "You pulled it out there at the end. I have to be impressed."

He scowled at my hand. "What? Are you an old man or something?" He curled his fingers into a fist and then pushed it toward me in invitation.

"It's traditional to shake the hand of the winner." But I bumped my fist to his.

"That's weak sauce. Let's go find the ice cream." He headed off in the direction of the concessions.

I turned to Jolie. "Weak sauce?"

"I think he's saying you're a loser, and not just in the literal sense." The way she was looking at me, she thought I was exactly the opposite of a loser and might even be about to tell me so.

I didn't want to hear it. Couldn't stand there while she

thanked me for being cool to her son, as if I was doing it for her. Or him.

And saying it was about me didn't make sense even to myself.

So I made sure she didn't get a chance to speak. "We better catch up with him before he needs a credit card."

I took off after Tate, not waiting for her to go first.

Twenty minutes later, we were sitting in a booth with two sundaes (me and Tate) and two beers (me and Jolie).

"Are you going to finally tell me why I'm here?" Tate scooped up a spoonful of his sundae, making sure to include lots of chocolate sauce before putting it in his mouth.

I could feel Jolie tense from across the table. When I looked at her, I could see it too.

Tate, who was sitting next to her, didn't seem to notice. "Because you were clearly surprised to see me, and then I found out you didn't even have your phone all night."

I'd been curious about his arrival myself, and now I realized exactly what must have happened. "Carla," I guessed, wondering if Tate had assumed it was me.

He put his spoon down. "That's what I thought. But why would she want—?"

"We can talk about it later, Tate." Jolie plunked the cherry off his sundae and brought it to her mouth, and while it was distracting to watch her bite into the juicy fruit, I wanted to have the conversation now, suddenly curious what she'd tell him.

"Don't put it off on my account." I finished off my beer, then raised my hand to signal the drinks girl to bring another.

She shot me a glare. "You know how Carla is..."

I almost felt bad for Jolie, having to juggle whatever stories she'd told her son with the fact that I was sitting right there in front of him.

But not bad enough not to stir the shit. "She broke into your phone and pretended to be you texting Tate? That's a new brand of bitch for Carla. Usually, she's a stand-by-and-watch-the-fire-burn kind of gal. Not a start-the-fire herself kind."

Jol chewed her lip, probably deciding how to navigate the mess before speaking. "I think she just wanted to see how you've grown up. She was around for the first seven years of your life, you know. She had to be curious."

"Then why didn't she just tell you to invite me? And why didn't we just keep in touch with her?"

"I've told you—my father and I are estranged. Keeping in touch with Carla would mean keeping in touch with him, and I didn't want him to know where we were." Her tone was tight, and there was no questioning she thought this should be the end of it.

I had a feeling Tate got the message but just didn't care. "Were you scared of him or something?"

She fidgeted nervously with the salt and pepper shakers on the booth table. "I really don't want to talk about this right now."

"Did you fight with him because he kicked Cade out?"

Jolie's neck went red, and I saw her debating whether or not to grab that as an excuse.

Obviously, she hadn't told her son much about her father at all.

It wasn't my place to interfere.

No matter how many times I told myself that, I couldn't quite latch on to it. Every time I looked at Tate, all I could think was *If he were my kid...* I'd never felt that way about a teen before. Or a child of any age, for that matter. I'd never wanted to be woven into a person's DNA the way I wanted to be woven into Tate's, and it was truly fucking with my head.

So much so that, even though I knew it wasn't my place, I went ahead and acted like it was. "Your grandfather is a monster, Tate. No other way to say it. An abusive, fucked-up asshole."

"That's it. Conversation over. We should get going." Jolie started gathering the napkins strewn across the table as if she were cleaning up to go, neglecting that neither Tate nor I were finished with our sundaes and that I had another beer on order.

She was on the inside of the booth, though, so Tate would have to stand up to let her out, and he wasn't budging. "Abusive?"

Admittedly, it wasn't just that I wanted to have an impact on this kid. It was also the resentment I felt toward Jolie that had me poking holes in whatever story she'd told about her past. Or as it seemed, *hadn't* told. It gave me a sense of power in a relationship dynamic where I was otherwise insignificant. "You know what a sadist is?"

"Cade!" Her tone was sharp and warning. "He's a kid."

"He's nearly seventeen. That's practically a full-grown adult." I gave her a glare as sharp as her words. "And don't tell me you didn't know the meaning at his age, in action if not the word."

She clamped her mouth shut, probably because she couldn't refute it without outright lies, and anything she said to clarify or smooth over would be an admission of truths she didn't appear to want to share.

Tate pressed on despite his mother. "It's a sex thing, right? Sadists are people who get off on pain."

My spine stiffened. Sex had generally not been a component of Stark's punishments. I didn't talk about the one time he had brought his pleasure into it. It was too humiliating. Too shameful. I'd never told a soul.

But we were talking in a general sense about Stark, not specific. "Pretty much, yes. In some relationships, the pain inflicted is consensual. No judgment if that's your thing—"

"Oh, my God." Jolie crossed her arms over her chest and sat back against the vinyl seat, her irritation displayed in a cute little pout.

"I'm not..." He shook his head, deciding to ignore his mother's reaction rather than address it. "And that was what my grandpa was into?"

"I don't know what went on in his bedroom, but I can tell you without a doubt that he derived pleasure from inflicting pain. Getting kicked out of that house was a blessing, not a curse. The terrible part was not that I left but that your mother wasn't able to leave with me."

I didn't want to know her reaction to that. Fortunately, the drinks girl picked that moment to deliver my beer, so I had a good excuse not to look in Jolie's direction while I dealt with payment.

After she left with my drink in hand, I studied Tate instead, watched his furrowed brow as he scooped ice cream into his mouth and worked the bits and pieces he'd collected into a picture of some sort. "He hit me, didn't he?"

Jolie's anger dropped instantly, concern taking over her face. "You remember that?"

He shook his head. "Not really. It just feels like I know he did." He angled toward her. "Why didn't you tell me?"

"You had counseling at first. The therapist said he thought

you were dealing with it well, and there was no need to bring it up unless you brought it up. We can talk about it later, if you want."

I tried not to feel left out. Not my kid, not my duty to be part of his emotional health. He was lucky, really. To have forgotten. Amazing what a mind could do in order to protect a growing child.

Too bad Jolie and I hadn't had the same method of coping.

"Is that why we left?"

"Yeah, tiger." She brushed a hand through his hair, and he pushed it off with an irritated shrug. She did a good job of not being offended. "I vowed he would never lay a hand on you again."

"Makes sense, I guess." He took it like it was no big deal, and it probably wasn't to this teenager who didn't have fear branded into his everyday life. Or maybe he was blowing her off because he was unhappy that she'd kept these things from him, which was understandable.

Either way, it was a real gift she'd given him—one not every mother gives her children, despite it being their job—and I suddenly wanted him to know that. "You would have had a very different life if she hadn't gotten you out of there. Whatever you might feel about her not telling you, and whatever struggles you may have experienced being raised by a single mom, she rescued you from hell. No other way to say it."

He looked at me with somber eyes. "Okay," he said, and though it was only two little syllables, I could tell he understood the seriousness of the facts if not the complete story they told.

He scooted to the edge of the bench, leaving an undeniable

space between him and his mother. A beat passed in silence. Then another.

He didn't speak again until he was scraping at the last of the chocolate in his bowl. "I guess what I don't get is why you two went back there then. If he's so horrible."

Jolie sighed, and I could feel the weight of it like it was my own. I couldn't imagine the burden it must have been over the years to carry the remnants from her past while caring for a child.

It pissed me off all over again that she'd thought she'd had to do it on her own.

Pissed me off mostly because it was easier than feeling hurt.

My own feelings aside, her son had a question that likely was not an easy one to answer. It was one thing to make sure he knew what kind of man his grandfather was. Quite another to tell him what his mother had wanted to do about it.

I considered letting her address this one herself, but she didn't jump to explaining, and I could see from her posture that she was weary from the stories.

Without ever having a kid of my own, I knew that I was a transparency-and-no-bullshit kind of parent, and even so, this wasn't the place to be completely honest. "We bumped into each other unexpectedly in New York," I said, selling the lie we'd sold Carla. "After a bit of reminiscing, we decided to go back to the house."

"That doesn't make any sense."

No. I was sure it didn't. "When you've suffered the kind of abuse that your mom and I did, it haunts you. Sometimes the only way past it is to face it head-on. Does that make sense?"

"Sort of."

My skin pricked at the judgment in his tone. "Hey, Tate." I

waited until I had his eyes on me. "You can't judge the choices she's made. You weren't there. You don't know."

He shrugged in response, obviously not wanting to let go of his irritation.

Yeah, I knew the feeling.

He might not have understood her, but I sure as hell understood him. Understood how anger was easier than forgiveness, anyway.

To be fair, his feelings likely extended beyond the secrets about her father to the secrets about *his* father. There might be a real chasm between them when she finally told him the truth.

What if he never had to know?

Was it selfless for me to consider that or selfish? Or just plain stupid?

Not your place to consider it at all.

"We shouldn't stay there tonight," Jolie said decisively after a short but heavy silence.

"We could get a hotel." I pushed my beer away, ready to leave it only half gone.

"Yeah. That's..." Her shoulders sagged. "Dammit. I didn't get a chance to put the keys in the office."

"We have to go back for our things anyway." Maybe she could return them quickly then, though after being caught in there the night before, it might not be quite that easy to slip in without Carla's notice.

Tate looked up from his phone. His ice cream gone, and at least some of his questions answered, he'd been texting for the last few minutes. "Will your dad be there?"

Jolie shook her head. "No, he's at his cabin. We were planning to leave tomorrow before he got back."

"We might as well stay then." There was defiance in his tone, as if he was daring her to insist otherwise.

Instead of answering, she looked to me to back her up. Tate looked to me as well.

Part of me wanted to earn points with her because I always wanted to earn points with her. Another part of me wanted to let her down.

Another part of me wanted to sneak her to the bathroom and fuck her against the wall. Fuck her mean. Fuck her a little sweet too.

It was confusing to be so conflicted.

So I chose my response without factoring in my feelings about her at all. "We should leave first thing in the morning. You two can take the beds. I'll sleep in the den." I made sure she understood my reasoning. "We may need the night to get the keys back in place."

Plus, we still hadn't made a decision about what we were doing next. I didn't want to cut off our access to the house just yet in case we needed it.

Her nod was reluctant. "All right. You're right. We should go then."

"I'll meet you outside," Tate said, holding up his phone. "I need to make a quick call."

Jolie's brow lifted in curiosity.

"The girlfriend?" I asked before taking another swig from the beer I'd meant to abandon.

"Yeah." He gave an embarrassed smile and slid out of the booth, bringing the phone up to his ear as he did.

"Girlfriend?" Jolie called after him in surprise. "What girlfriend?"

Before she could chase after him, I put an arm out and stopped her. "Leave him be."

I braced myself for admonition. I'd been crossing the line for the last hour, and she'd yet to call me on it.

Instead of letting me have what I deserved, she let out a breath. "I just didn't know he had a girl."

"Not usually something a kid wants to talk about with his mom, even when their relationship is a good one."

She scrutinized me, as though she was unsure why I continued to try to reassure her. Or why I tried to do anything nice at all, for that matter.

Fuck if I knew myself.

"You're good with him," she said, and now I wondered if I'd been off base about her thoughts. Maybe she'd gone in an entirely different direction.

I hesitated.

Because what I wanted to say was that I could have been better for him. I could have been *there* for him, if she'd let me. Despite not sharing DNA.

I could be good with him in the future.

I could be good with her, too.

But that would mean I'd have to take my own advice—stop judging the choices she'd made. Stop holding on to my resentment. Stop picking apart the past.

And while I'd accepted I'd do pretty much anything for her, I wasn't sure I was capable of doing that.

TWELVE
CADE

It was almost ten when we got back to the house. It was dark, but the porch light was on, which I would have attributed to habit before the conversation with Terrence.

Now, all of my mother's actions felt suspicious. Was the welcome gesture a ruse?

I left the car idling. "She wouldn't have called him, would she? Let him know we were here?"

I expected Jolie to brush off the idea right away. Instead, she chewed her lip and considered. "She helped me and Tate leave. It wouldn't make sense for her to turn on us all of a sudden." But she didn't make any move to get out of the car.

In the back seat, Tate leaned forward, poking his head between us. "There aren't any new tire marks on the snow. If he's here, where's his car?"

Good point. Tate's Versa was blocking the empty side of the garage, so there wasn't a vehicle hidden in there.

I looked again at Jolie to be sure.

She let out a tense laugh. "He's not here. We're paranoid. Come on." She pushed open the door and got out.

"Paranoid? Scarred is more accurate." I was talking to myself since Tate had gotten out too.

I turned off the car and followed after them. Whither she went, so did I, it seemed.

Still, after everything, she had me on a fucking leash.

Whatever had motivated my mother to leave the light on, she'd had to consciously leave the door unlocked, and it was. No one greeted us when we stepped inside, but I knew for sure he wasn't there. The air felt thick, but I could breathe. Stark had a presence that smothered, even from rooms away.

Tate picked up the duffel bag that he'd left inside the door. "Upstairs?"

"The room at the end of the hall," Jolie said, then turned to me. "I think I'll take a shower."

It could have been an invitation. Yesterday, I'd have taken it as such. Part of me still wanted it to be—a big part of me—and I had a feeling that I could easily change her mind if it hadn't been.

But I was afraid she'd take fucking as a sign that things were settled between us, and I wasn't sure I was ready for that.

Her son only a handful of feet away didn't make it a good idea either.

"I'll come up with you to get my things."

I could see her lip twitch, the urge to say something more, but whatever it was, she let it pass with a nod.

A few minutes later, with my bag in hand, I found my mother watching some crime procedural in the den, dressed in a zip-up robe, her feet curled up underneath her. She reached for the remote as soon as she saw me and turned it off with a click.

"You don't have to do that on my account." Not that I planned to stay in the room if she did, but there were other places I could be.

"It's over anyway." She stood up, her eyes landing on my suitcase. "You'll keep up appearances for the boy but not for me?"

Her wounded act would never have worked on me. Tonight it had a particularly sour taste. She'd driven the car while her husband had abducted a teenager. She'd possibly done more. Any chance of excusing her as another of Stark's victims had been erased with that knowledge, and now I could barely look at her. "I can sleep in the living room, if you'd rather."

She let out a huff, irritated that I hadn't picked up on her cue. "Here is fine. I can get you bedding."

"You still keep linens in the hall closet?" I waited for her to say yes. "I can get it myself then." Anything to get rid of her. If I didn't, I'd tear into her with accusations, which might feel good in the moment but wasn't in our best interest. If I wanted the investigation against Stark to come through, I couldn't let her see our cards.

Thankfully, she took the hint. "Good, then I'll be off to bed myself. You're still leaving in the morning?"

"Unless you think your husband will be back sooner."

"He won't be back until afternoon."

"Then we'll be sure we're gone by then."

She gave a nod, then started to leave.

I let her get past me before the niggle inside me grew into

something I couldn't ignore. "I'm not asking why. I'm not demanding anything you should feel the need to defend. Just answer me one thing—you know he's a bad man, don't you?"

She had the nerve to look angered by the question. Then she almost blew me off but at the last second turned back. "I never wanted you here, Cade. Not back then, when the only reason I sent for you was because he demanded it, and not now. Take that however you will."

I stood in the same place for several minutes after she left, not dissecting her words but convincing myself I didn't care. Whatever message she meant to give me, I did not care. I did not care. I did not care.

Said enough times, maybe I'd start to believe it.

It took all of two minutes to grab a blanket and sheets, having decided not to bother with the pull-out bed. The couch would be fine, not that I expected to get much sleep. The ghosts were too present tonight. It had been different last night, with Jolie distracting me from them. Without her, they were every-where, filling every corner of my mind.

I managed to avoid them by concentrating on every sound in the house, waiting to be sure that Carla was asleep before returning the keys we'd stolen to the office. Pretending that was all I was listening for and not straining for signs that Jolie might still be awake.

What would it matter if she was? Nothing good would come from going up those stairs. Not a goddamned bit of good.

As convinced as I was, the temptation and the memories kept me restless. For the next hour, I paced the den like a lion in a cage, wishing I had a punching bag to direct some of my energy. I took my boots off. Texted Donovan, who didn't respond. Did fifty push-ups. Stood perfectly still when I heard a door close upstairs.

Silence followed, and any wish that she might be sneaking down to see me vanished when five minutes passed, and I was still alone.

I wished I hated her.

After her betrayal, it was almost possible.

But if I really hated her, I had to be done with her, and if I was done with her...

I wasn't sure I could ever be done with Jolie. Seventeen years had gone by, and I hadn't been able to let her go. Would it really be any easier now?

Maybe the things she had left to tell me would help push me away.

In which case, I wasn't so eager to hear them.

It was close to midnight when I felt confident that my mother was truly asleep. I managed not to glance up the stairs at all on my way to Stark's office. The door was still unlocked, so it only took a couple of minutes to return them to the place Jolie had told me she'd gotten them from. I made sure to latch the lock on my way out.

Then, because that was off my plate and all my bandwidth was available to fixate on her, I climbed the stupid fucking stairs.

It can be like old times, I told myself. Sneaking in to be with her, but through the door instead of the window. We could leave the lights off. We wouldn't have to say a word. Just burn off some of the tension like animals in the night.

At her door, I grabbed the handle, then changed my mind and lifted my fist to knock.

Then thought about how little I had left to lose to her, and that got my head in the right place.

I let my hand drop, turned around, and went back down the stairs.

This time, when I got to the den, it wasn't my mother waiting for me. My deliberation at her door had been in vain. She hadn't even been in her room when I'd stood there. I hadn't heard her when I'd been in the office.

Jolie sat on the couch, wearing nothing but the T-shirt she'd stolen from me, her hair tousled from being left to dry naturally, her lips wet from the run of her tongue. In the soft glow of the one lit lamp, she could have been an angel if I didn't know she was a temptress.

Maybe I did hate her after all.

Hated how she owned every single part of me, from my heart to my pride. Hated how I wanted to hurt her and heal her all at the same time.

"Are you here to talk, or are you here to fuck?" I asked, my cock already hardening behind the zipper of my jeans.

She stood to face me, and there was something in her eyes—a window of sorts—and for a moment, I thought she might actually be ready to tell me all her secrets. Thought she might push to put everything on the table and see what was left between us, when all I wanted at the moment was to be with her.

But she surprised me when she spoke. "I'm here for whatever you'll let me have."

I closed the distance between us, on the verge of letting out a laugh until I realized none of this was the least bit funny. "I'm feeling mean, Jolie. Do you want that too?"

My hand settled on her throat before she'd answered, so I could feel her swallow and the rush of her pulse.

I squeezed ever so slightly, so her voice was strained when she spoke. "I want it all, Cade."

No sooner than her consent was past her lips, my mouth crashed against hers, hard and aggressive. I kissed her like a thief—taking, taking, taking. Barely giving her a chance to breathe. Pushing my tongue into her throat when her kiss came too easily. Biting her lips. Sucking them raw.

I'd been so gentle with her in the past. I hadn't known how to fuck rough, and even if I had, I hadn't wanted to ever show her anything but kindness.

Now I touched her like it was punishment. For staying with him instead of going with me. For letting him have more of her life than she'd given me. Maybe if I'd hurt her then, she'd have chosen differently. Maybe she needed to be bullied into her love.

They weren't fair thoughts—they definitely weren't thoughts I'd have outside the moment—and as out of control as they felt, I still couldn't make myself truly hurt her. I couldn't even bear to put enough pressure on her neck to leave bruises despite the fact that she was practically asking for it, pushing her throat up against my hand, whispering, "More," whenever I gave her a chance to speak.

I was as mad at my inability to damage her as I was at her ability to damage me. I fought against that reality, trying to take some of that power for myself, and the next time I had her lip between my teeth, I bit hard enough to taste blood, only to soothe it with a gentle swipe of my tongue.

With a frustrated growl, I wrapped my hand in her hair and pulled her away from my mouth, pulled her downward, to the couch. Her legs opened slightly, and I could see she'd come to see me without any panties on. Had she never really planned to talk, or did she just know what I'd choose? Either answer fucked me up inside.

Yeah, I did hate her.

Roughly, I wrenched one of her legs up over the arm of the couch, spreading her into an uncomfortably wide position, then dropped to my knees. Without any preamble, I began lapping at her cunt. Lapping like a dog that had gone days without water. Like her sole reason for existence was to provide for me.

"This doesn't feel very mean." She was breathless, her back arching, giving away that her words were a lie with the way she quivered from the cruel assault.

But if she was going to taunt me...

I sucked her clit hard. Hard enough that she gasped.

Then she started to beg, her body jolting as I added teeth. Alternating between nips and sucks, I took her quickly to the brink.

Just when she was about to go over, I broke off entirely.

See? I could be mean.

I ran my fingers along her inner thighs, pinching her skin until it was bright red as she bucked her hips toward me, urging me back to her cunt, which I only returned to when I was good and ready.

Then I repeated the attack, winding her up, backing off abruptly, until she was crying and pleading and drenched with sweat and pussy juice.

But I wasn't even mean enough to deny her an orgasm forever.

As soon as I shoved three fingers inside her, she erupted. I didn't even need to push in with a second stroke. It would be easy and cruel to demand another one from her right after, which made the idea tempting, but my cock was a fat steel bar, and I chose it for my next weapon.

She was still shuddering while I worked the shirt over her head and hadn't recovered by the time I got my jeans down and my cock covered with the condom I'd retrieved from my wallet. Limp as a rag doll, she was easy to manhandle, and I moved her how I wanted her—pulling her ass up to the arm of the couch, yanking her to the edge so I could shove inside her balls deep.

"Oh, God," she moaned as I drove in.

She was slippery but tight, and I didn't give her a chance to adjust before pummeling into her. Her breasts jiggled from the impact, and I liked that—liked seeing her out of control too—so when she moved her hands to hold them, I smacked them away and increased my brutal tempo.

Hard, hard, hard, over and over, and it still wasn't enough. Wasn't mean enough.

I straightened one of her legs against my torso and pushed forward, bending her as far as she could go, and gripped one nipple, pinching at it until she whimpered and arched her back, trying to ease the pain.

"You want it all, Jolie?" I was in her face. "I would have given it all to you. I would have given you everything."

"Give it to me now."

It pissed me off, how she could plead so sincerely for something she'd once thrown aside.

Pissed me off more that I couldn't stop myself from giving.

Still pinching her breast with one hand, I shoved my other fingers in her mouth—three of them. The same fingers that had been inside her. I fucked her mouth with those fingers as savagely as I was fucking her cunt, until she was drooling and choking, and still, when I gave her a second of reprieve, she again begged for more.

"You're so fucking greedy. How much is enough for you? Should I take your ass too?" She couldn't respond—I shoved my fingers farther down her throat when she tried—but she gave no sign of resistance, and that made me mad too.

Because I wanted an excuse.

I wanted something I could point to that would prove this couldn't work between us.

I wanted to be able to accuse her of giving up, like she did back then, because if she was going to break my fucking heart again—if she was going to destroy me like she so very much had the power to do—I wanted it done sooner rather than later, when there was still possibly something left of myself to salvage from the wreckage.

But she didn't give me that excuse.

And when I finally pulled my fingers out of her mouth so I could pull her other leg up against my chest as well, she looked me dead in the eye. "I want you, Cade. All of you. I won't give you up this time."

She was crying, I noticed. Truth be told, I might have been crying too. "You have me. You already fucking have all of me." She clenched tight on my cock, but I didn't slow my assault. "No, you don't get to push me out now. You asked for it, and now you have to take it."

And she did.

Took all of it.

Even though I fucked her like I was trying to tear her apart—and maybe I was, and maybe it was too rough—but when she whimpered my name, she was still asking for more, and when she came again, it was a whole-body orgasm that shook through her like an earthquake, wrecking her completely.

Wrecking her as thoroughly as she always wrecked me.

I came right after, groaning and grinding into her with an orgasm that reached every end of me—to the tip of every finger, down to my toes, up my spine to the top of my head—and held on for long seconds, as if I was indeed giving her everything I had, everything I was. Everything until there was nothing left of me alone, and all that existed was the me that was part of her.

It was freeing to feel linked to her like this, and with my eyes closed, I imagined that when I opened them again, I would somehow see the joining. That we would be soldered together with alloy. That our bond would be obvious to anyone.

Of course, that wasn't the case. We were united only by my half-hard cock, still buried inside her pussy, and the tear-stained woman that laid depleted beneath me was not only separate from myself, but someone I had just selfishly used.

"Are you okay?" I let her legs fall to the floor and drew her to me. "I shouldn't have... Did I hurt you? I'm sorry. I'm so sorry, baby." I spattered kisses across her cheeks and nose, so intent on delivering my apology that I barely recognized she was giving one of her own.

"Stop. Don't say that. I loved it. I'm the one who's sorry. I'm so deeply sorry."

I pulled back to look at her when I realized her apologies had nothing to do with what had just occurred, and for once, I was able to hear it. Suddenly, I could believe that the years she'd spent without me had been a torment for her, that the ache inside me was shared. That we were on the same side. That we'd always been on the same side.

I kissed her. Desperately. "How could you think that I wouldn't want both of you?" I cradled her face between my hands and stooped so she had no choice but to see me at eye level. "I would have been his father. Even if you didn't love me, I would have loved you enough for the both of us."

Fresh tears sprang in her eyes. "I loved you too much to saddle you with my baggage."

"The weight of being without you is heavier than any baggage you could have put on me."

"I didn't know. I didn't know." She started to break down, but I wouldn't let her, kissing her until I was her focus, and not her guilt. Forcing her to be here with me instead of locked inside whatever prison waited for her in her head.

We'd both been locked up too long.

We both deserved to fly away. Together, this time.

With my hands still on her face, I pushed my forehead to hers. "I won't lose you again, Jol. I hurt right now from every secret you've kept, but this hurt feels better than the hell of being without you."

"I don't deserve you."

"You better fucking try. Because I'm not letting you go again, whether you want me or not."

She smiled, but it brought another round of tears. "I want you, Cade. I've always wanted you. There's nothing I've ever wanted but you."

"I mean it." I brushed the wet from her cheeks. Crying and sex-rumpled and wrecked, she'd never looked so beautiful. "You're stuck with me from here on out."

"Stuck is my new favorite." She brought her hands to my neck and gripped on as tight as if she was drowning, and I was the only thing keeping her afloat.

If she was going under, fuck, so was I.

As if she could read my thoughts, she trembled. "Are you scared?" I asked.

She shook her head. "'Sink or swim, baby.'"

Except this time, I wasn't wrapped around her like an anchor. This time, our heads were both above water, and I was pretty damn sure I could see the shore.

THIRTEEN
JOLIE

After several more lingering kisses, Cade took care of the condom then cleaned me up with the T-shirt I'd worn.

"Now I have nothing to wear when I go back upstairs." Obviously, I'd steal another of his shirts.

"Guess you'll have to stay down here."

"Well, it was either that or take you up with me, but with Tate down the hall..."

He chuckled. "As if you don't know how to be quiet."

Even after what we'd just done, it made me blush to think about how I'd had to learn to keep my pleasure inside all those years ago, afraid we'd be heard. "And we got caught anyway."

Too late, I worried that I'd said the wrong thing, that I'd sent him down the path of darker memories, and he'd go cold again.

He did just the opposite. "You're so beautiful," he said, staring at me with hot eyes that reminded me that I was the only one of us who wasn't wearing any clothes.

I shivered from the intensity of that stare, but he must have assumed I was cold since the next thing I knew, he pulled me off the arm of the couch where I was perched and wrapped a blanket around the both of us. "There's less room down here than in the twin upstairs, but I promise I'll keep you warm."

"Skin to skin would do that job best." I slipped my hands under his sweater, but he caught me at the elbows before I could try to take it off.

"We both know where that would lead, and you're still catching your breath from the last round."

I didn't have a chance to respond before he was kissing me again. No wonder I couldn't catch my breath. I wasn't complaining.

And when he pulled me with him to lie on the couch, I didn't complain about that either.

For long moments, we lay like that—stretched out, face-to-face—sometimes sharing deep kisses. Sometimes just looking at each other. It had been so long since we'd been wrapped up together, and now that we were, I couldn't imagine how we'd survived so long apart.

I'd only made it through because I'd had Tate.

How had Cade managed?

Thinking about it made me too regretful and sad, so I pushed those thoughts away and did something I hadn't done in years—daydreamed about our brighter future.

"What are schools like in Tokyo?" I asked, tracing the curve of his lip with my finger.

He thought about it a second before realizing why I was asking. "You're not moving to Tokyo."

Panic rose quickly in my chest. We'd just said we weren't letting each other go. "Your company is—"

He cut me off. "I can work at whichever office I want. I'm an owner. I don't have to work at all, if I don't want to. I get a portion of the profits no matter what, and it's more than enough to take care of us quite comfortably. I don't need the salaried position on top of that."

"But I'll move to Tokyo if that's what you want."

"I want us to decide what we do together. What do you want?"

It had been so long since anyone had asked me that. The last person who had might have even been him. "Honestly? I just want you."

He gave the smallest smile, but it lit up his entire face, and then of course I had to kiss him. Or he had to kiss me. Whichever, we were kissing again.

God, I'd forgotten how nice it was to just kiss and be held. There'd been men from time to time over the years, but only one came close to being serious, and no relationship had felt this intensely affectionate. Like we were teenagers all over again.

"We're going to have the academy to think about," he said when he eventually broke away. I must have looked confused because he clarified. "When your father gets arrested, the school is going to be yours."

"I hadn't thought of that." How had I not thought of that? I'd based my career choices on that one-day possibility, even after I'd left him, assuming that one day I'd be left everything.

Of course, that had been before my last encounter with him, when I realized he would cut me off entirely. "He'll give it to Carla," I said.

"She doesn't have any interest in running it. Trust me. She

wouldn't know where to begin. And after today, it sounds like there's a good chance she'll go to jail too."

That was weird to think about. It had to be weirder for him than for me, and I started to say something that would allow him to talk about that if he wanted, but he'd read my mind and shook his head before I got any words out.

So I stayed on topic instead. "Whatever happens, he'll leave it to someone else."

"You're his only living relative. Who else is there?"

"He'll give it to charity. He's already told me he's not giving me anything of his. He'll sell it, and donate the money." I let out a sharp laugh. "No, he'll use the money for his legal defense."

Cade didn't blink. "Then I'll buy it."

"You will not—"

"You're right. *We'll* buy it. I'm not used to thinking in the plural."

I was too happy to refute him. "We're really a we now, aren't we?"

"Yes. We really fucking are." He placed a kiss on the side of my mouth. "We could have our wedding here. On the grounds. That would piss your father off to no end, wouldn't it? Replace his legacy with ours."

"You're planning our wedding now?"

"We'll go all out. Make it huge. We didn't think we'd ever be able to be public, but fuck that. Unless you'd rather not have anything to do with this place."

"No, I love this place." I rethought that. "I mean, I love parts of this place. I love the you parts. I hate the him parts."

"We'll get rid of all the him parts."

Years had passed since I'd truly known Cade, but I knew

him well enough to know that he didn't make idle plans. He meant the things he said.

Suddenly, my chest didn't feel big enough to hold what was inside of me. "Is this your way of asking me to marry you?"

He shook his head. "No, no, no. I'm not doing that again. Not without a real ring. The fake one didn't take so well."

I giggled because he made me feel dizzy and light. I still had that pipe cleaner tucked away in a jewelry box.

And then I sobered up because there was also so much between us that was still unbearably heavy. "It took the first time, Cade. I just—"

This time, he cut me off with a kiss. "Later, okay?"

I got it. He didn't want to talk about Carla. He didn't want to talk about the past. He wanted to be here, enjoying the present. Planning the future. Blotting out the bad stuff.

That had been the way with us back then too, and in the end, that might have been to our detriment. If we'd been honest about what had been going on—if *I'd* been honest—maybe everything would have been different.

I worried that we'd get stuck in that same bubble this time too.

"We *will* talk about it," he assured me, reading my thoughts. "But not here. We need to be on neutral ground when we do. There are enough ghosts around us here."

"Okay."

He ignored the reluctance in my tone. "Tate still has another year and a half before he graduates, doesn't he? We probably don't want to uproot him before that."

It was a good distraction. Hearing him talk about my son was fucking sexy. "He's really happy where he is."

"And there's the girlfriend. We wouldn't want to break them up."

I playfully slapped his shoulder. "Who is this girlfriend? I haven't heard a word."

"I think it's a new thing. He's still feeling her out. He'll tell you. When he's ready."

A knot pulled in my belly. I had things I had to tell my son, and I didn't think I'd ever be ready for this truth. "I have to tell Tate."

I could tell he knew what I was talking about when the corners of his mouth fell downward.

"I know—we're only thinking about good things right now, but I can't let myself dream so much that I end up putting this off. I have to tell him soon."

"Do you?"

"Yeah. It's not fair to have kept him in the dark this long. Each minute he spends with you, he thinks he's getting closer to his father."

Cade brushed my hair away from my face then caressed my cheek with the pad of his thumb. "So maybe you don't tell him at all. Maybe you just let him keep this one lie."

"You don't know what you're offering." I wasn't considering it yet—that would be a whole other thought process that required some deep evaluation about whether or not I still wanted to be the kind of mother who could lie to her child.

Right now, though, I was only thinking about Cade and the weight of what he was suggesting.

He propped his head up on his hand. "I think I do."

I mirrored him. "This is the kind of thing you can't decide on a whim. You'd be tied to him. Forever."

"What is it you think we've been talking about here?"

I blinked. "We've been talking about you and me."

"And he's part of you. You're a package deal. I'm well aware of that."

I shook my head. "No, this isn't the same. You can leave me. You can't—"

He wrapped his hand around my jaw. "I can't leave you, Jol. It's not happening."

"I know, but—"

"I should have been his father. In practice if not in blood. You should give me the chance now that I should have been given then."

That got me in the gut.

Before I could process enough to say something, though, he spoke again. "Think about it. You don't have to decide right now."

I couldn't decide right now even if I wanted to. Making those kinds of plans required everything on the table. This was why the past had to be discussed. It kept popping back up whether we wanted it to or not. Our future didn't exist without the past. They were also a package deal.

I tucked the blanket around my bare chest, as if that would make me feel less vulnerable, and sat up a little more. "We should talk about that, Cade. What happened. Why I didn't go with you back then. About Tate's father. It could change how you feel about us."

He sat up as well, moving so he was sitting next to me.

Side by side made the conversation safer somehow. Because we could look straight ahead instead of at each other. Looking in his eyes was what felt most dangerous.

"First of all, we have enough on our plate right now planning what's next. With your father, with us." He took my hand

in his and laced our fingers together. "Second—and most important—it's not going to change things between us. What part of
I'm not letting you go do you not understand?"

When I'd let him go all those years ago, I'd given up on any
chance of ever having him. The possibility of us still felt so
unreal, and admittedly, it was going to take a whole hell of a lot
of talking about it and seeing it happen before I could really
believe it in my bones.

I knew that. I understood that about myself.

What I didn't understand was how he could believe in us.
"I just don't know how you can trust me." I swallowed,
surprised by how much this meant to me.

"And you think I'll trust you more once you've told me
everything you need to tell me?"

"I think I'll be more trustworthy when I don't have any
more secrets."

"Yeah, I suppose you will be." He turned his head toward
me but tilted it down toward my shoulder instead of my face. "I
know trust matters. And maybe I'm not quite there yet, but you
aren't either, or you wouldn't be worrying about me."

"But..." I didn't know where I was going with that, only that
it hurt not to have his faith, which I knew I had no right to ask
for, and I wanted to believe that everything we were saying
tonight had a chance of being real.

What was the point of any of these words?

I repeated what he'd said only moments before. "What is it
you think we're talking about here?"

He opened and closed his fingers around mine. "I think
we've been talking about our future. Do I trust that you mean
it?" I felt him shrug. "I know that *I* mean it. And I know that
even after what happened in the past, I still want you. I still

love you. Try as I might not to. So the way I see it, I have two choices: I can either not trust you and be alone and miserable forever like I've been for the last seventeen years, or I can try to trust you and maybe get everything I've ever wanted. Either way, I still love you. Seems my odds are better if I stick around."

My vision blurred. It was more than I deserved. So much more.

I twisted to face him. "You really still love me?"

"I think it's pretty fucking obvious."

"I really still love you too."

His breath seemed to catch. And then he was cupping my cheeks, bringing my mouth to his for a salty kiss. "It wouldn't matter if you didn't. I'm still not going anywhere."

"But I do. So much."

"I'm going to give you everything, Jolie." We spoke between kisses that were getting progressively deeper. "Everything you ever wanted."

"You're what I've wanted."

"A real family."

"A baby?"

He pulled away to see if I was serious. "Tate's almost grown up. You want to do it all over again?"

"With you, yes."

"I want that." He grinned. "I want a baby with you, Jolie, very much."

"I'm thirty-five, though, so we should get on it soon."

The next kiss took us back to a prone position. This time, when I tried to take off his sweater, he helped me get it off. He stood to get out of his pants, and then there he was, standing like a naked god, pumping his hard cock in his fist.

Be still my heart.

"We could start right now," he said, looking at me so fiercely I could have gotten pregnant from his gaze. "I don't have to put on a condom."

"Condoms aren't only to prevent pregnancy." It was the kind of decision that shouldn't be made in the heat of the moment.

On the other hand, if he was clean, I didn't really have to think about it. "I haven't been with anyone except you in more than a year."

Damn, I sounded pathetic. I knew he'd been with someone else as recently as last week.

"I haven't been bare with anyone but you, Jol. Ever." Another stroke of his cock, and I didn't know if it was his words or his actions that had my stomach flipping. "Tell me now because I need inside you."

I nodded.

Was still nodding when he stretched out beside me. He put a hand on the side of my neck, firm and sure, but nothing like the last time when he'd put pressure on my airway. I'd been really turned on by that version of him.

This version of him took me to another plane of existence.

He pulled me snug up against him. I lifted my knee to his hip, and immediately, I could feel the thick crown of his cock nudging at my entrance. I tilted up in invitation just as he pushed forward, sliding in easily like a key in a well-oiled lock.

"Cade!" I threw my head back in pleasure, fighting against the instinct to close my eyes. I wanted to see him. Wanted to see everything he said without words. Wanted to see how I affected him. Wanted him to see how he affected me.

He kept hold of my gaze, kissing me reassuringly. "I'm right here with you, baby. Me too." He threaded himself in and out of me, slowly, making sure every stroke was felt by every part of my insides. "Fuck. It's incredible. You feel..." He finished the sentiment on a low growl.

"I know." He felt hotter without a condom separating us. Skin to skin with our most intimate parts. I was already clenching around him. "It's good. It's really good."

Another kiss. I loved that he was a kisser, that he was reaching to me with his mouth as often as I reached for him.

He was restraining himself, but I couldn't tell if it was for me or for him. And then he asked, "Was it too much? Before?"

"No, I loved it. I wanted it." I shivered as he hit a particularly sensitive spot. "But this..."

"This is special," he finished for me.

I had to blink back tears. Shit, I was an emotional mess. "This is love."

He surprised me with a shake of his head. "This is trust. I'm completely vulnerable right now. Completely bared."

I clung harder to him, digging my fingers into his back when he adjusted his angle and hit me even deeper. "It's love, too," I insisted.

"Yeah. It is."

We stayed like that, him rocking in and out of me, whispering I love yous, both of us clutching to each other. Trusting each other. Loving each other. If we didn't conceive a child tonight, we were still planting something new. Something that would grow. Something that would bind us forever.

Whatever came tomorrow, whatever our future brought, neither of us were going to face it alone.

FOURTEEN
CADE

The first thing I was aware of when I woke up was my phone buzzing.

The second thing was that Jolie wasn't in my arms.

Trying to ignore the panic of her absence, I checked who was calling then answered. "About time you checked in."

"It's not even nine yet," Donovan said, sounding like he'd been awake for hours. Likely the man never slept. "I figured you'd still be sleeping."

"I figured I'd hear from you last night." I pulled the phone away to check the exact time. Eight thirty-seven. The alarm I'd set was due to go off in eight minutes. "It's not like we're under a time crunch here."

"Forgive me for having my own long-lost love to woo."

"God, no. I can't picture you wooing." In my mind, Donovan's version of the term looked more like a kidnapping and hostage situation.

"I get it. The kids never like to think about their parents having sex. Daddy won't talk about it anymore."

"Fuck, don't. Do not ever refer to yourself as Daddy again." I shuddered.

"I think I just proved my point."

"Can we please get to what you've found out?" The longer we stayed in this house, the more my skin itched. It didn't help that I'd woken up alone.

"Not a lot, but enough. Leroy said the investigation is real top secret, but he let me know that he feels pretty good about it. They apparently have an informer and tabs on the girl who went missing before Thanksgiving, Cassie Benito, and they haven't made their move yet on Stark because they want to be sure they can get her out before anyone gets tipped off. But it's looking like an any-day-now bust."

I waited for relief to sweep through me, something that I wouldn't truly be able to feel until we were gone. "In other words, it's time to get out of here."

"That would be my advice."

I scrubbed my face, trying to wake up enough to get me thinking what was next.

Donovan was ahead of me. "Are you wondering if you should still plant the drive?"

That was exactly what I was getting to. "An informer doesn't necessarily mean the deal is sealed."

"It was a different situation when you tried to press charges," he said, knowing exactly what I was thinking. "The FBI wouldn't be involved if they didn't have something more solid. With that said, you know what I'd do."

Donovan didn't let anything happen without being sure it

would happen how he wanted it to happen. He'd still plant the drive.

I'd promised Jolie I'd destroy the motherfucker, and for that reason, I was leaning toward D's thinking.

On the other hand, I was feeling...good. For the first time in a real long time. Vengeance wasn't as high on my priority list as it had been a few days ago.

"I'll leave it up to Jol." This had been her show from the beginning. I wasn't going to take over calling the shots.

"Pussy. Oh, while we're on the subject. Hold on a sec." The sound muffled, but I could hear him saying something to Sabrina about naked breakfast in bed, an indicator that this call needed to be over ASAFP. "Whatever you decide," he said when he returned to me, "let me know when you're ready for me to set up an appointment for that new tattoo of yours. Nate has a guy if you'll be back in the city soon."

That goddamned tattoo bet he'd made with me only a week ago. He'd said I'd be in bed with Jolie before the week was out, and if I was wrong, he got to pick my next tat.

"Fuck off," I said. Wasn't Sabrina enough to occupy him? He still had to keep his fingers in my business as well?

But I supposed it was his need to meddle that had gotten us this far, so I thanked him for the information and told him I'd keep him updated before I hung up.

Awake now, I stretched and sat up. Except for my state of nakedness and my T-shirt wadded up on the floor, there was no trace that Jolie had spent the night in my arms. I might have thought I'd dreamed it all without that bit of proof. Had that really happened? Had she really told me she loved me? Did I really fucking believe her?

Fool that I was, I really fucking did.

I was eager to go find her, not completely because I doubted anything that had happened, but also because I wanted to spend as little time apart from her as possible.

First, though, we had to work on getting out of the house before Stark showed up.

I dressed quickly, stowing yesterday's clothes in my suitcase, and was folding the blankets I'd grabbed from the linen closet when I became aware of someone in the room behind me.

I was smiling when I turned, expecting to see Jolie. Instead, I found Tate, rumpled but awake, already wearing a snow cap as though he was headed out. "We're ready to go when you are."

"Your mom send you?" Why hadn't she come herself? I told myself I wasn't worrying, but it was a lie. She'd burned me before. It was only natural that our new status felt fragile.

"No, she's doing her hair. I'm supposed to be loading up the car—which I did—and then I thought... I don't know. I guess I was just wondering when you wanted to take off."

He was nervous, too, I noticed now. Of course he was. He thought I was his father, and I hadn't yet acknowledged him as my son, and here we were getting ready to head out, and the poor kid probably didn't have any idea where that left us.

No wonder Jolie had been fretting about him last night. This was a big thread to be left dangling.

I ran my hand over my beard, trying to decide what I could say to make this better for now without stepping on his mother's toes. Things said in the dark didn't always hold as much weight in the light, and I thought about the offer I'd made. Tested whether I still meant it when I said I'd be his father if she'd let me, and I wasn't surprised to realize I still did.

I hoped she let me.

But that was her decision to make and not one I could pressure her into, so I'd have to give different assurances to Tate for the time being. Which wasn't hard because, regardless of what I was to him, I had once been a teenager whose mother had brought a new man into my life. I knew what it felt like to have no power in that situation.

Whatever else I was allowed to give him, I could at least give him the opportunity I never had. "I'm ready any time," I said, "but listen, Tate. I'm glad you came back here. I had something I wanted to talk to you about."

He perked up like I'd just offered him the keys to Donovan's Jag. "Yeah? Sure. What is it?"

"Well." I leaned against the arm of the couch, careful not to remember how I'd had Jolie propped up there while I'd fucked her the night before, hoping the reduction in my height made me a little less formidable. "I wanted to let you know that I am..." I hesitated, not because I was unsure of what I wanted to say, but because it was the first time I'd declared it out loud to someone other than Jolie. "I am very much in love with your mother. Always have been, to be honest. We'd lost each other for a while there, and now that we've reconnected, I'd very much like to be in her life. In your life, too. If that's all right with you?"

He blinked a few times—his excitement wasn't so palpable —and I had a feeling he was getting choked up. "Yeah, yeah." He cleared his throat. "That would be all right with me. Does Mom know?"

My smile came easily. "Yes. I've discussed it with her."

"Oh. Okay." He shifted his weight from one foot to the other. "And did she say anything to you? About me?"

I knew what he was asking and quickly choreographed my own dance around it. "Some. I'm eager to learn more. Like I said, I want to be in your life as well as hers. I don't want to take her from you, and I don't want you to feel like I'm only interested in her. Though, I know it can be hard letting a stranger in, especially at your age. I certainly didn't have a good experience with my stepfather."

"Stepfather?"

Fuck. I saw the natural leap he'd made after I'd said it. It was what I intended to be to him—if not more—but that was jumping too far ahead. "I just meant... Well. Maybe eventually. Or not... Look. I was trying to relate as best as I can."

I sounded like an idiot.

I wiped my sweaty palms on my jeans and straightened to my full height. "The point is, I really want you to be okay with...um, me. Being around."

He returned my grin. "I'm okay with that. For real." His eyes drifted somewhere behind me while he considered something. "My grandfather was really that terrible, wasn't he? Like I know he was. It would just help to have some details?"

I nodded.

He had a right to know, didn't he? He'd been a victim himself, even if he didn't remember it very well, and Stark was part of him, awful as that was to think about.

But opening up about the details was a fucking hard ask. Jolie and I hadn't even ever talked about it. Not really. We knew we were both suffering, and that was enough. It wasn't any wonder that she hadn't wanted to tell her son about it.

I would tell him, I decided. I would take the burden from her, if she needed me to, but that had to be her choice. "We'll talk about it," I promised. "But not today. In the meantime, I think you should ask your mother about it."

"Yeah. Okay."

"And don't feel like it has anything to do with you if she has a hard time talking about it, okay? It's going to be a hard conversation for her. She carries a lot of hurt from that man."

He nodded, and I knew he understood when he spoke next. "I hope that means you'll be extra careful not to hurt her too."

I'd spent so much time concerned with how she'd hurt me that imagining the flip side was possible almost made me laugh. "She's lucky to have you, kid. And I would do absolutely anything for your mother. Anyone who hurts her, I will take them down, including myself if necessary. I promise."

"Good. I'll hold you to it." He looked down at my suitcase, possibly searching for a change of subject since this one had gotten so heavy. "Is this ready? Want me to put it in your car?"

That was a good question. Mine was the rental, and whether or not I held on to it for much longer depended on what happened next. "I'd appreciate that. Thanks."

"Anytime."

I let him get a head start, eliminating any more awkwardness he might feel by my presence, then followed after him to the front of the house and then went upstairs where I assumed Jolie was still getting ready. I slipped into her room—my old room—without knocking and found her bent over, ass in the air, tugging on a boot.

"What a lovely sight," I growled.

She twisted her head to give me a mock scowl. "Predator."

"If you're the prey, then definitely yes." I pulled her into my arms before I thought about it too hard. She hadn't showered, and this close, I could smell the faint whiff of sex on her, and it was all I could do not to press her against the wall and fuck her again right now. "I woke up without you."

She placed her palms on my chest. "I wanted to be there, trust me. I didn't think Carla would appreciate walking in on us naked on her couch."

"Might have been fun to scandalize her, though."

"I was more worried about Tate," she admitted.

"As long as you still..." I didn't know how to finish it, so I trailed off, letting her assume an ending.

"Oh, I still. All of it." She tipped her chin up, begging to be kissed, but when my mouth was an inch above hers she asked, "You, still?"

"Every single word." I pressed my lips to hers, and the commitment she'd made in words was verified with her kiss, a kiss that went on a little too long, and by the time I pulled my mouth away, my pants were uncomfortable.

"How did we ever manage to keep our hands off each other?" I stretched the distance between us so our bodies were no longer flush, but I held on to her waist.

"Then or this past week?"

"I don't think we actually managed this past week. Then, well, I suppose your father was deterrent enough."

"Yeah." Her body sagged at the mention of Stark, and I hated that he still had that effect on her. Hated that I couldn't make everything disappear just by holding her in my arms.

At least I could give her some good news. "Hey, I heard from Donovan." Quickly, I filled her in on the status of the FBI investigation and what I'd learned from my earlier phone call.

"So we don't have to plant evidence," she said when I'd caught her up.

"It couldn't hurt, I don't think. But it sounds like they have a solid case without it." I tried not to let my preference show in my tone so that this decision would be all hers.

She looked down at her hands as they played with the collar of my flannel button-down. "Is it terrible if I just want to walk away right now and never look back?"

"Why would that be terrible?" It was a fucking relief.

"Because I dragged you into this, and everything you've done so far, like coming here, would be a waste of—"

I cut her off. "None of this past week has been a waste." I lifted her chin so she would look at my eyes. "I'm walking out of this house with you. And with Tate. There is nothing more I could want or hope for, so don't even go down that road of regret. You hear me?"

She took a breath in, her chest stuttering as she did. Then she smiled. "I love you."

"Just keep telling me that." I kissed her quickly. Then again. Then not so quickly.

When her arms snaked around my neck, I knew I had to come to my senses before our clothes ended up on the ground. I pulled farther away from her this time but held her hands in mine. "I'm guessing Tate needs to be in school tomorrow. And you as well?"

She blinked, as though she'd forgotten the world that existed outside of our bubble. "Yes. I suppose we do."

"Okay then. I'm coming with you to Boston." I wasn't asking. "We can figure out what's next from there."

She was beaming now. "All right. There's got to be a place to return the car in Hartford. We could meet there and then drive the rest of the way together."

It wasn't a bad plan, but I'd already thought this through. "Actually, I was thinking I'd return the car in Boston."

Her forehead creased in question.

"It's only a two-hour drive, and I thought you might want the time alone with Tate."

"Oh." She let go of my hands, taking a step back, and I hoped it wasn't because she thought I'd overstepped with the suggestion. "I haven't..." She started again. "Did you really—?"

Again, I interrupted. "I said I meant everything I said last night, and I really do. Even that. I will be his father, in whatever way you'll let me, and you don't have to decide that right now. But even if you leave that for later, he needs to hear something about me from you. About what you want me to be in your life. It's not fair to just bring me in without that conversation."

"Ah, fuck. You're right." She ran her hands through her hair. "I can't believe I didn't think about that. You must think I'm a terrible mother."

"God, no." I closed the distance between us. "Never. I'm elated that you're as wrapped up in me as I am in you, and the only reason I'm letting you out of my sight for two seconds is because I don't want anything to fuck up what's going to be between us—between *all* of us—including starting off on the wrong foot with him."

"He's going to be happy about this, you know."

"I know." She gave me a suspicious look. "I might have already laid the groundwork with him."

"What did—?"

"It doesn't matter. You can talk to him, and when we meet up in Boston, we'll go from there."

I would never get tired of her adoring gaze. "Did I mention that I love you?"

"I love you, too, baby." What I meant was I love you more,

but that wasn't relevant. "We should get going. Your father might have gotten an early start, and we don't want to be here when he shows up."

Fifteen minutes later, after Carla had given them a stiff goodbye, I put Jolie in the passenger seat of Tate's Versa with a promise to follow soon behind. I wanted to do a final sweep of the house first to be sure there wasn't any evidence of our visit, and I supposed I wanted to be alone for my own goodbye with Carla.

Not *wanted*—needed.

She'd been as much of a hanging thread over the years as Jolie had been, and while I was now certain I wanted to follow Jolie's string, I was also certain I wanted to cut my mother's completely.

As if she suspected as much, she was waiting in the foyer when I walked back into the house. "Langdon called while you were out there. He's on his way home. Should be here in less than an hour."

"Good thing I'm about out of here then."

"Yes, quite good. You don't want him to find you here."

My curiosity got the better of me. "What would he do if he did?"

"Probably kill you."

"And you'd let him?"

She stared at me indignantly, as though she couldn't believe I'd need to ask.

I couldn't believe she thought I already knew the answer.

"Never mind," I said, realizing I probably didn't want to know.

I also realized there was nothing more I needed from her. There wasn't a loose end here. I'd already put her in the past, and when I walked out that door, if I never saw or heard from her again, I wouldn't be disappointed at all.

Without another word, I brushed past her upstairs to do my final walk-through and then back downstairs to check out the den.

I found nothing. We'd left the place as we'd found it. As though we'd never been there. As though we hadn't found ourselves again inside these walls.

The house was perhaps a harder goodbye than my mother. I hadn't gotten a real chance for one the first time I'd left, and this time…

It should have been easier to part with this place, with all its haunted memories. The problem was that, as horrible as those memories were, I couldn't separate them from the moments that I'd had with Jolie. They came together—the good and the bad. Without one, there wasn't the other, and I wouldn't trade anything for what I had with her. Not even the hell that we'd been through.

But that hell was over now. Only heaven on the horizon.

The sooner I got to that horizon, the better.

When I came back to the foyer, my mother was still in the spot I'd left her. "Are you going home with her?"

I considered what answer I wanted to give her. She wasn't important enough to be considered an enemy any longer, but she didn't deserve anything satisfying. "It doesn't matter," I told her eventually. "None of us are your concern any longer."

She stuck her chin out defiantly. "Tate's phone number had a Massachusetts area code. And it only took him a couple of hours to get here. That doesn't make it hard to guess where they're living."

My back went straight. "Is that some kind of threat?"

She held her stance for several seconds before she sighed. "I don't know what it is, Cade. I was trying to point out that I already know more than you want me to know, so does it really matter if I know anything else?"

"I'm going home with her." I only told her because I wanted her to realize I'd be with Jolie going forward, in case she did mean her statement as a threat. "I'll be staying with her from now on." I'd have a really good security system installed if Jolie didn't have one already.

"All right then." She looked like she wanted to say more, but I didn't care enough to pry it from her.

I turned to the door, and maybe it was easier when I wasn't facing her because she spoke to my backside. "There's one thing, Cade, that you should know."

Jesus, not this.

I couldn't take anything she had to offer—an explanation, an apology, a final defense. Whatever it was, it wouldn't be enough, and if it wasn't enough, it wasn't worth hearing.

Telling her as much was a waste of energy.

Without acknowledging the remark, I put my hand on the doorknob.

"It's about Tate's father. Did she tell you who it is?"

How she was able to find the one weakness she could exploit, I had no idea. Maybe she'd learned from her husband.

I debated. Told myself to leave. Told myself the answers were waiting for me, already on the road to Boston, as soon as I was willing to hear them.

But if they were already waiting for me, what was the harm in hearing what it was that Carla thought she had to add to the conversation?

I turned my head toward her. Then my whole body. Didn't

say a word. I refused to give her more than that. I shouldn't be giving her even this.

"I let myself believe he was yours," she said. "Because I wanted him to be, I admit that. It was naive. But if he's not yours, then it has to be..."

Shit, I was exhausted. "Spit it out, Mom. It has to be...who?"

"My husband."

FIFTEEN
JOLIE

A month ago

MY HEART TOOK off at a gallop with the sound of a door banging shut in the kitchen. I hadn't heard the garage open—a sound I'd been listening for—but Carla had mentioned that it had been replaced recently. Apparently, the new one was whisper quiet.

I shouldn't have had feelings about that, but I did. The whine of the old one had frequently acted as an alarm, telling us my father was home and to be en garde. Even though it had been years since I'd lived in the house, the missing siren felt like a victory in his favor. Just one more way that he could control the lives of those around him. Keep them on edge and unaware of when he'd next return.

It was only Carla living here now, of course, but I was definitely on edge at the moment.

This was a bad idea. I shouldn't have come.

The only movement I made was to strain my ears, listening for conversation that would verify his presence.

"Whose car's outside?" he asked.

Carla's voice was too hushed to hear her response, or maybe I wasn't trying hard enough since my head was suddenly distracted with paranoia. I'd taken the train and rented a car so that he couldn't trace my license plate, but with my father came unreasonable fears. What if I'd forgotten something? Had I left my rental receipt with my information on it in the front seat? Had I locked it? I could picture him opening the door and sniffing around, never mind that whoever owned the car might think it a violation. It was parked in front of his house, and that was all the permission he needed.

Anxiously, I found the key fob in my pocket and clicked the lock button. The beep that sounded meant it had already been locked.

That was good. Still, I didn't feel relieved.

And I wasn't at all ready when a moment later, the kitchen door swung open, and there he was, tall and looming, as formidable as ever.

I scrambled to my feet, an automatic act of respect that I immediately regretted. I'd told myself I'd carry myself with confidence. He didn't have any power that I didn't give him and all the other sorts of mantras therapists had given me over the years.

They seemed easier to believe when he wasn't standing in front of me. Now my knees were shaking, and though I hadn't tried to use it yet, I knew my voice wasn't all there.

He stared at me for what seemed like an eternity, and I couldn't help wondering about what he saw. How mad was he about the dyed blonde hair? Did he notice the fifteen pounds I'd gained since I last saw him? Did he prefer me with the curves?

I was disgusted with myself for caring, and yet I couldn't deny that I did. Despite everything he'd done to me, not as intensely as I'd once cared, but blatant enough to have to acknowledge. I shouldn't have expected less. The desire to please him was so ancient within me that I often wondered if it had been the first part of me to form when I was still a cluster of cells in my mother's womb.

No, that was the lie he'd convinced me of.

I didn't really want to please him. *He* wanted me to please him, and he'd groomed me to believe it was my choice instead of the other way around.

But I could tell myself that all day, and it still wouldn't feel any different standing in front of him. Wherever the desire came from, it was there, and it was persuasive, so when his lips curled in revulsion, I felt the shame he meant me to feel.

"You have some nerve showing up here." He hadn't even bothered to take his coat off. His careful, meticulous self had been shocked enough by the announcement of my presence to forgo his coming-home routine. That should have felt like a win. "What's it been? Eight years now?"

There was a trick here somewhere. Had he really not cared enough about my absence to know how long it had been, or was he trying to throw me with his air of disinterest? Was he trying to figure out if I knew the correct answer?

Like always, I found myself questioning my response, as if it might be tied to a punishment.

He doesn't have any power that I don't give him.

I gave the truth. "Ten years."

"A decade. Well." He wore a satisfied smile when he looked me over this time, and I couldn't decide if that meant I'd said the right thing or the wrong thing. "I suppose you aren't here for a social visit."

I shook my head.

"Of course not. To my office then."

I felt the color drain from my face. "I'd prefer we stay here to talk."

As soon as I'd said it, I knew I'd fucked up. Letting him know what I wanted gave him the upper hand, and he didn't hesitate to play it. "The dinner table is for eating. You're more than welcome to stay for a meal, but if you want to have any real discussion, it will take place in a room suited for such."

I looked helplessly to Carla who stood behind him, as if she had any ability to save me. Her blank expression was a reminder for how to school my own as I pondered my choices. If I said no, this conversation was over before it started. If I said yes, he'd win the round. But maybe that would make him more amenable to losing the next?

I knew right then it was a lost battle, no matter what I did. That I should march out the door without another word, and never look back.

If I'd come for myself, I would have.

But I'd come for Tate.

"Lead the way," I said, surprising myself with the steadiness of my voice. It didn't have to be a lost battle. I'd known how to appeal to him at times in the past. I could find a way to appeal to him now.

Whatever bravery I'd found to follow after him, it left me at his office door. I stood on the threshold, watching him as he took a seat behind his desk, unable to move my feet any farther.

This room had been a place of torture for as long as I could remember, and while I tried not to bring the past to mind, countless atrocities played out before me. They rolled together. A snatch from one incident layered with a scrap from another, turning a lifetime's worth of memories into a short reel of terror.

It's just a room, I told myself.

Standing in the hall wouldn't erase the things that had happened inside the room. Walking in willingly might even help me take back some of what I'd lost every time I'd walked in by force.

It was complete bullshit.

"I'm moved to see you hesitate, Julianna. It appears you consider this place as I do—special."

He was trying to goad me, and it worked. I stepped into his lair. "If by special you mean should be burned down, then yes. I do feel that way."

He let out a patronizing chuckle. As though he thought me adorable, and I hated myself for giving off that appearance. Adorable meant vulnerable. Vulnerable meant able to be hurt.

"We haven't even begun the discussion, and you've already moved to hostility." He clicked his tongue. "This might be a fun evening after all."

He'd changed. Once upon a time, he would have pretended he didn't find any delight in the things he did to me. Now, he was brazen enough to flaunt it.

I TOLD myself it was courage on my part—not fear—that dared to not close the door behind me when I crossed to the chair in front of him. Dropping my purse on the ground next to me, I sat down, keeping my spine straight.

He eyed the open door with an eyebrow raised but didn't fight me about it. I told myself that was another win for me and that it meant I was safe.

Stupid me, I felt the need to test it. "Careful. You'll give Carla the wrong idea."

"My wife respectfully stays out of my business, whether the door is open or not."

My stomach dropped until it felt like it was hanging between my knees, and I had to coach myself calm. Just because he thought that was the case didn't make it true. She wasn't completely devoid of humanity. She'd helped me leave. She'd help me again if I needed her.

I hoped to God she wouldn't get the chance to prove me wrong.

Before I could get my wits enough to drive the conversation, my father spoke again. "I'm sure you have an agenda, Julianna, but considering how you left without a note or warning or forwarding address, I believe I should be allowed to ask some questions. Where are you living these days?"

I shook my head, half in response to him and half to myself. I'd already lost any advantage I had by surprising him, and I had no idea how to take back the reins. I'd vowed to myself that I wouldn't tell him anything about my life, and I intended to keep that vow, but I hadn't expected to be grilled. Which made me an idiot because of course he'd grill me.

"You don't think I have a right to that. After all this time. What are you afraid I'll do with that information?"

Come after me. Hurt me. Hurt Tate.

Honestly, my fears weren't even that tangible. I didn't really expect him to get in his car and drive to Boston and torment us. I didn't want him to know where I was because I didn't want him to exist at all, and that meant he couldn't have access to me in any way, shape, or form.

When I remained silent, he poked again. "I at least deserve to hear about Tate."

Red flashed before my eyes. He didn't deserve shit, and I had to fight the urge to tell him exactly that. It was only because that was what he expected that I was able to bite my tongue.

"Actually, Tate is the reason I'm here," I said, seeing the opportunity to take the wheel. I swallowed the bad taste, ashamed of myself for using my son as bait even while knowing it was the most sure way forward. "He's a very smart kid with a promising future. I'm pretty confident he could make it into one of the best schools for college, though probably not with full rides. You know how little financial aid covers, and I don't have the means to pay the difference."

I tried to give as little details as possible, leaving out that Tate was hoping to study engineering and looking specifically at MIT. He could live at home then, which would eliminate the expense of room and board.

"Of course he's a smart kid. It's in his DNA."

He was complimenting himself, but I knew he wanted me to say thank you, and the words slipped out before I had a chance to think about them.

It didn't earn me any points. "That's pretty ballsy of you, don't you think? Showing up here after a decade to ask for money?"

I'd expected this, and I managed to remember the come-back I'd prepared. "No. I think it's pretty reasonable. Legally, you have a responsibility toward him."

"Is that a threat? Because the statute of limitations is in my favor."

"Yes, you made sure to keep me under your thumb until that expired."

"I'm sorry that's how you choose to view my love and care."

I bit back a laugh and reminded myself that riling him up wasn't the way to get what I was after. "I'm not threatening you, Dad. I'm here because you promised to take care of him, and I have faith you'll live up to your word."

"Is that right?" His smile was smug. He knew the tactic I was playing, which meant it was a failed move. Flattery had always been the way to win his favor, but not if he didn't believe it was genuine. "I seem to remember that promise came with the agreement that you'd stay here."

"The agreement was that I wouldn't leave *then*." I couldn't bring myself to mention Cade, afraid I'd be too emotional if I did. "I didn't realize it relied on me staying forever."

"That's why you should have had a conversation with me about it before you took Tate and ran away. I have rights where he's concerned, and as he's not yet eighteen, those rights have definitely not expired."

Now *that* was a threat.

He wouldn't follow through, would he? Admit to everyone his relationship to my son?

I ran through the logic behind it in my head. Too much time had passed for him to be arrested for what he'd done to me, but his reputation would be destroyed. The school would have to close. He wouldn't allow that to happen.

Which meant I could use it against him. "Go ahead and claim those rights then. I dare you."

He almost looked proud when he smiled this time. "I

wouldn't want to drag Tate through the scandal, and I doubt that you would want that either."

"No." It was why I hadn't gone that route already. "So let's stop with the threats and just focus on him. A good education is what he needs, and I'm asking you to provide that for him. That's all. Nothing more."

"You want me to write you a check and just let you leave with it? No questions asked?"

Ideally. "That would be great."

"How about this." He stood up and casually circled around in front of his desk while every muscle in my body went on high alert. "I'll pay for Tate's education in full. If he graduates from Stark Academy."

"Oh, no. No. No." The suggestion alone made me want to scream.

He leaned against the desk, unbothered by my refute. "We're a prestigious school, Julianna. Only the top kids in the nation make it in. He'll get into any college he wants with us on his transcript. This is the offer of a lifetime."

"No, not happening. Not a chance."

"You don't want good things for him after all? What if I promised he could stay in the dorms?"

I didn't even take a beat to consider. "There's no way in hell I'm letting you anywhere near him. Ever. You got that?"

"Ah, so you don't really want what's best for him. You want what's best for *you*."

Despite my better instinct, I let him get to me with that. "Fuck you." How many times had he pretended what was best for him was really best for me? "You're a hypocrite to say that to me, and you fucking know it."

"The mouth on you. You used to always be so prim and proper—yes, sir, no, sir. Where did that come from? I like it."

My stomach curled, and this time I nearly choked on bile. "This was a mistake." I picked up my purse off the floor and stood.

But before I could take a step toward the door, he'd grabbed my arm.

"Don't touch me," I snarled. I tried to pull away too, but he held me too tightly. A panic that I hadn't felt in years spread through me like a wildfire in the brush, and since there was no longer a chance of me controlling what showed on my face, he knew exactly what was going on inside me.

There was no doubt that he liked that, too. "You don't like that option, princess, then I'll give you another." He wrapped his other arm around my waist and wrenched me closer. So close my face would be mere inches from his if I wasn't leaning back as far as I could, and I didn't have to ask what his other option was because it was very much implied.

It was also crystal clear that he wasn't really giving me the option. "You can keep struggling, if you want," he said, his eyes dark. "You know it will go fast if you cry."

"You disgust me." I disgusted myself as well. Tears were already falling, and I could feel myself turning back into the girl I'd always been with him—a girl who didn't fight back. A girl who knew there was no escape. A girl who had learned that fighting only drew it out longer.

No. I wasn't that girl anymore. I was a full-grown woman. I was a mother. I was not his to use and defile and humiliate.

I lifted my knee, intending to aim for his crotch, but he closed his thighs tight around mine, restricting my movement. "The more you fight me, the more I want to hurt you."

He would, too. He'd hurt me in so many vile ways that I'd come to prefer the rape. Sometimes, I'd even believed that I should be grateful for it. I was ashamed of how many times I'd thanked him afterward. How I'd even thought that it was somehow a show of his love.

I was ashamed now that I'd thought the same man who'd raped and abused me for years might have had enough heart to help take care of Tate.

I was such an utter fool.

But I still had a free hand. And whether it was foolish or not, I brought it up to his throat and squeezed. As hard as I could. Digging my nails into his skin and pressing against his airway.

"Let me go!" I screamed, knowing it was futile. He was bigger and stronger than me, and when he wrestled out of my grip, he'd make me pay, but I put all my energy into it, and when he let go of my other arm so that he could pull at the hand choking him, I added it to the effort, squeezing and squeezing and squeezing until he punched me so hard that I saw stars, and my grip loosened involuntarily.

Before I got my balance again, he'd grabbed both my wrists.

"Langford?"

He froze at the sound of Carla's voice. I turned my head to find she was standing in the doorway, and though she managed to not look surprised at what she saw, she did look intent.

"Not now, Carla," he said, a dismissal.

Help me, I said with my eyes.

She barely looked at me, but she didn't leave. "Dinner's ready. You won't like it if it's cold."

He took another several beats to make his decision. When

he finally let me go, he did it with a push, sending me to my knees. "Perfect timing. Julianna was just leaving."

I scrambled to my feet, then backed away from him, afraid to take my eyes off of him before I made it to the door. Once I did, Carla made room for me to pass by without actually looking at me. "Sorry to hear that. I'll be sure to clear up the extra place setting."

Maybe it was the best she could do without getting herself punished. She'd most likely suffer later for her intervention, and maybe I should have felt grateful to her for that.

But the only thought in my mind as I drove away was too loud and persistent to drown out everything else, and I committed to it fully before I considered the consequences or whether or not it was even feasible—one way or another, my father had to die.

SIXTEEN
JOLIE

Present

WE ONLY MADE it fifteen minutes before I made Tate pull over so I could take over driving.

Once I was behind the wheel, I turned off my phone, wanting to model appropriate driving behavior, then reassured him as I pulled out into traffic. "It's not that I don't trust your skills behind the wheel."

I cringed at the lie. It was exactly the reason I'd made him switch places. "I mean, you're a good driver. I just have more experience, and the roads are slick."

"I drove down here without a problem." It was impossible to tell how upset he really was since his general teenage demeanor was sullen, even when he was in a good mood. "Seems that should have been enough to prove myself."

"That was different."

"Because you hadn't wanted me to come?"

"Because I hadn't been in the car with you." I reached over and slapped his feet down from where he had them propped on the dashboard.

Now he scowled at me. "It's my car!"

"That I pay for."

He harrumphed. Then he turned up the radio and curled up as much as his long body allowed, his head facing the passenger door. "I'd rather you drive anyway. I'm gonna sleep."

I considered letting him. His weekends were usually spent sleeping in, and even though it hadn't been me who had requested his presence in Connecticut, it had been because of me.

Plus, I needed to talk to him about more than just Cade's role in my life, and I was dreading it. Putting it off another few hours was tempting.

But procrastinating made it harder and harder to want to tell him the truth at all. And maybe it was for the best that I didn't. Why not take Cade up on his offer to keep up the ruse? I'd already been lying to my son for years. If I hadn't brought Cade back into his life, Tate would have never known he wasn't really his father.

Except that wasn't true either.

Eventually, Tate would have gone looking for Cade. He'd already done an internet search, and telling him he'd found the wrong guy would have blown up in my face when he got serious about his hunt. He would have realized the Cade he'd found had been the one in my life. A paternity test would be ordered...

I shuddered thinking how Tate might have discovered the truth.

With Cade's offer to step into the role of father, that potential disaster was averted. I should grasp onto the suggestion and let Tate continue to live a sheltered life.

It was what I wanted to do.

Nothing would have made me happier.

But the weekend back at my house had taught me there was no escaping my past. It didn't matter how much I ignored it or ran from it or kept it from my son—it was still there, buried under the foundation of my being, a fundamental element of who I was.

Having Tate there had made the lesson learned even more poignant. Less avoidable anyway. Tate shared that history, and if he ever decided he wanted to know more—especially when my father was arrested and his life was scrutinized—what Tate could discover would be terrible and shocking.

It would be better coming from me.

And it would be best if I didn't try to pick and choose the secrets to keep and admitted everything.

I turned down the radio. "Before you drift off—"

"Too late. I'm already asleep."

"You're talking pretty clearly for someone who's asleep."

He groaned but turned his body so he was upright. Or as upright as a sixteen-year-old ever was when riding in a car. "What?"

"We should talk about your father." There. I'd said it. There was no going back now.

"Oh, I already know."

I glanced quickly at him in alarm. Cade wouldn't have told him the truth, and Tate's face was too passive to suggest that he'd somehow figured it out. "You know...what, exactly?"

"About you guys. Like, it was obvious anyway, the way you

keep giving each other those starry-eyed lovebird looks. And Cade's suitcase was in your room, so I'm guessing he slept in there the night before I arrived."

"You saw that." It wasn't a question. More of a statement of acknowledgment on my part. An embarrassing acknowledgement. I could feel my cheeks go bright red. "I didn't realize you noticed."

He made an annoyed sound and followed it up with one of his favorite phrases. "I'm not dumb."

I somehow managed to refrain from rolling my eyes and tried to figure out what parental thing I should be saying. Not having dated much during his life, Tate wasn't used to seeing his mother as a woman, and I hadn't prepared how to talk to him about it. "That was probably awkward for you to see. I'm sorry about that."

He did roll his eyes. I could feel them rolling without looking. "Mom. I'm not twelve. I get how the birds and the bees work. Remember that uncomfortable conversation that one day after fifth grade? Trust me, I know about sex."

Immediately, I wanted to know exactly what he knew about sex and how well he knew it, as well as who he might know it with, but I remembered Cade assuring me that Tate would tell me when he was ready and forced myself not to ask.

"Okay. Well. Okay." If he wasn't going to be embarrassed about my sex life, I could try not to be as well. "Glad you understand."

"Anyway, he told me he's going to be a part of our lives now and all that, and that's cool with me."

"Oh. He said that?" More and more, I was feeling I did not have the upper hand in this discussion.

Tate shifted in his seat. "Yeah. This morning. He said he was coming home with us and asked if I'd be okay with that."

That must have been what he'd meant about laying the groundwork. "And you are? Okay with that?"

He was quiet, and when I glanced at him, I found him studying his thumb, wearing a contemplative expression. "I'm okay with it for me, definitely. I guess I'm a little worried that you might not be okay with it for you, though."

I considered his thought process. He wanted to get to know the man he thought was his father, and that made sense. But why he thought I wouldn't want Cade around was a mystery to me. "I want him with me, Tate. I really do. I've never gotten over him, and I'm...well, I'm a little scared to have him back in my life, but just because relationships are always scary, and I'm out of practice with them. But I'm willing to take that risk because of how I feel about him and because I think he feels pretty strongly about me too."

"No, he does." He turned his head in my direction. "He told me he's in love with you anyway." Now he blushed.

God, what a character. Sex didn't faze him, but emotions got him flustered. It was sweetly innocent somehow, and if I hadn't been driving, I would have wanted to give him a hug or ruffle his hair.

Which would have annoyed him, so it was probably for the best.

"So you knew how he felt. Were you worried I might not feel the same?"

Out of my peripheral vision, I saw him give a one-shoulder shrug. "You just so rarely do anything for yourself, it seems. So if you're inviting him into your life because you want him to be there, then I think that's a really good thing for you, but if you're inviting him because you think that's what I want, then I'm going to feel really guilty about it."

My chest tightened. He was a thoughtful, caring kid, and I was bursting with pride about it, but now I also worried that I'd been too selfless in my child-rearing. Had I really made it seem like everything I did was for him? On the one hand, that was what a parent was supposed to do, wasn't it? My father certainly hadn't, and I'd promised myself I wouldn't be like that, but maybe I'd gone too far in my efforts and put a different sort of weight on my child's shoulders.

God, parenting was hard.

And I was good at overthinking. "It's not for you. I promise."

"Good." He grinned. "Then I'm really okay with it."

"It will be weird having someone else in our house. It's going to take some getting used to on both our parts, and if it's not working out for you, then you need to tell me, and—"

"We'll figure it out," he said, cutting me off before I once again offered to sacrifice my happiness. "I'm only around for another year and a half anyway."

I did not want to think about him leaving. So I didn't.

And I tried not to think too hard about how much damage could be done in a year and a half. Cade had only been in our household for a year, and that had completely changed the trajectory of his life.

Besides, Cade was not my father, and I was not Carla. "Yeah. We'll figure it out."

With that sorted, I tried to find another pathway back to my agenda.

Before I did, he spoke again. "Can I ask something, though?"

"Sure."

"If you both were so hung up on each other all this time, why did you ever get separated in the first place? Your dad kicked him out, right? But that didn't mean you couldn't keep in touch behind his back."

When I tried to look at the situation from his point of view, it seemed ridiculous. The easy answer could have been to blame it on poverty. Tate was a privileged kid in many ways—we'd struggled, but we'd never gone without the internet or a cell phone. Cade truly had nothing when he'd left, and explaining that to Tate was probably all he needed.

But that wasn't the truth, and I'd started this talk wanting to be honest. "It's complicated," I said. "And I'm not saying that as an excuse because I'm going to try to explain, but I'm also going to ask you to forget about logic when you're trying to under-stand because sometimes humans aren't logical, for a lot of different reasons, and that can make people seem really stupid, when in fact, some things are just *really complicated*."

"Uh...okay..."

Great preface, Jolie. Way to make things clearer.

I turned the radio from a low hum to off. "First, you should know, I had meant to run off with Cade after graduation. But then I found out I was pregnant with you." This didn't seem like quite the right moment to say that I'd been unsure of pater-nity, so I skipped that particular detail. "And I knew that if I left with Cade, we'd have nothing. No money, no healthcare, no family—and I didn't think that was the best situation to bring a baby into.

"And I didn't tell Cade that was why because I was afraid that if he knew, he'd try to change my mind, or he'd stay nearby, and I was pretty sure that if my father ever saw him again, he'd kill him."

"Literally kill him?"

I took a deep breath before I answered. "Yeah. He beat him up pretty badly as it was, and my father promised he wouldn't go after him if I stayed."

"He would have really gone after him?"

That was one of those questions that made me look stupid in retrospect. Feel stupid, too. "He said he would. And I believed him. That's one of the complicated things that's hard for me to explain because on the outside, it seems like I had so many other options. And I probably did. We could have gone to the police. We could have found a shelter. We could have tried to get the help of friends."

I paused for a moment, struck by all the ways I could have done things differently.

Then I shook off the regret. "But here's the thing about abusive relationships—the abuser wields all the power. I believed my father would do the terrible things he promised because he'd taught me time and time again that he would. It was impossible for me to see myself as capable of fighting back. I'd tried to report him in the past, and no one believed me, but my father knew what I'd tried to do, and I got punished for it. I got punished for anything and everything that I did that wasn't perfect, and after so many years of that, I had been trained to just try to make him happy. So it didn't matter if he would actually have gone after Cade—I believed he would, and that was enough to scare me into staying.

"And he was my father, Tate." I glanced at him and found him staring straight ahead, a slight frown on his face. "I thought he loved me. I thought that's what love was. I loved him too—

almost as much as I hated him. He was the person who'd raised me. I trusted him. Trusted that he'd be awful. Trusted that he'd come after me. Trusted that he would always have power over me. He broke me before I'd finished forming, and that kind of broken is really hard to fix. Does that make any sense?"

Another shrug. "A little, I guess. It's hard to understand."

"It is. I get it." A car passed me, and when I looked at the speedometer, I realized I'd slowed down while I was talking.

I resumed my speed before going on. "The other thing that comes with abuse is shame. It doesn't make any sense to blame yourself for what happens to you." Realizing I sounded like the text on a support website, I shook my head and rephrased. "I was embarrassed about the things he'd done to me. It felt like it had to be my fault. That there was something wrong with me, and so when Cade showed up, and my father hurt him too, I did feel less humiliated. Less alone, at least. But I still wasn't able to talk about it, and not talking about it meant that I never told Cade everything that my father was doing."

"Like...what?"

I could hear a rhythmic flicking sound, and when I peeked at him, I saw his foot was resting on his other knee, and he was picking at the sole of his shoe.

"You mean, what did my father do to me?"

"Yeah." *Pick, pick, pick.* His focus was glued to his sneaker.

"Well." It was a fair question. Abuse ran the gamut, and I'd been pretty vague in most references to it so far. "Physically. He hit. And whipped. He liked to slap me a lot, but he rarely broke my skin. Cade, on the other hand—he especially liked seeing Cade bleed."

That was Cade's story to tell, though.

I needed to stick to my own. God, this was hard.

"Mental and emotional abuse was his specialty. He would degrade me. Call me worthless and stupid. He liked to confuse me and manipulate me. And he, uh." They were just words. I could say them. "He would do sexual things to me. That was what I never told Cade. And I think that was another reason why I didn't run away with him. Maybe even the main reason. I was afraid he'd find out, and I was just so, so ashamed."

I'd talked about it a lot in therapy those first years after I'd left home. Discussed and analyzed until I'd felt like I'd gotten a pretty good handle on how to move on.

Then I'd put all those memories in a box, buried it deep inside of myself, and tried never to think about it again. I'd been pretty successful until I had gone back home a month ago. One little encounter with my father, and the box flew open, and the memories and self-loathing were as vivid as ever.

My eyes stung as the fog of shame shrouded me now, and I made sure not to look at Tate until I was sure that no tears would fall.

When I was certain I wouldn't break down, I looked at him again, only to find he was fighting his own tears. Less successfully than I had.

"Oh, honey!" I put my hand on his thigh and quickly found a place to pull off the highway.

As soon as I had the car in park, I took off my seat belt and stretched my arm awkwardly over to rest on his shoulder. I desperately wanted to pull him in for a hug, but he was almost seventeen and self-conscious of any vulnerability, and he was already leaning as far from me as possible as he pinched at the corners of his eyes.

I had to settle for patting his shoulder. "I didn't mean to

make you cry. Talk to me, can you? Tell me what you're feeling?"

He shook his head, refusing to look at me. "It's just... It just sounds really awful."

"Yeah. Yeah." I opened the glove box looking for a napkin or tissue and found only junk, so I shut it again. "Yeah, it was pretty awful. Which is why I haven't talked about it."

"But I wish I'd known."

"I know. I know." I *hadn't* known. It hadn't ever occurred to me that he would want to know. I was just talking, trying to say reassuring words. "I should have told you. It's hard to talk about. I didn't know how."

I remembered my purse on the floor in the back seat, and I reached in and dug around for a Kleenex while I patted his thigh. "I can tell you more, too, if you need me to. Not right now because this has already been a pretty heavy conversation, and I need a break from it, but if you need to know more in the future."

"Okay." He sounded choked up but less on the verge of breaking down.

Finally, I found a tissue, and he took it from me gratefully. He blew his nose, and once he was done sniffling, he said, "I'm sorry that happened to you."

"I am too," I said.

He looked at me—finally. "I suppose you want me to give you a hug now."

"I'd love one."

He took his belt off and reached his arms around me.

"I love you, kid."

"Love you, Mom," he mumbled.

He let me hold him for longer than he had in years, and

even though he was the first to pull away, I was sure the hug had been for him as much as for me.

In typical fashion, he handed me his used tissue. "Do I look like your trash can?" I teased.

He gave a slight smile then swiped it from my hand, only to toss it in the back seat. "I think I know enough now, if that's okay. I don't need any more details."

"It's okay." It *was* okay. For now, anyway. Telling him who his real father was would probably count as more details, and considering how hard this had been on him, I imagined that conversation was going to be a doozy.

That could wait, though. This had been more than enough for one day.

"You okay enough for us to get back on the road?"

This time, his grin reached his eyes. "Can I drive?"

"Nice try."

"Fine." He gave a fake pout and refastened his seat belt as I steered the car back onto the highway. "I guess while you're driving, I'll tell you something."

"Tell me what?"

I could feel his blush even before he spoke. "Well, you see, there's this girl..."

SEVENTEEN
CADE

I had every intention of driving straight to Boston.

Or maybe I had no intentions at all. My mind was a storm. My vision was bright red. I had a surreal sense of both not being connected to my emotions and also being nothing but emotion, and that emotion was rage, rage, rage.

Blinding rage.

I didn't remember saying goodbye to my mother, or if I even did. I didn't remember getting in the rental car or pulling out onto the drive. Like the day before when I'd grappled with the knowledge that Jolie had a son, I was aimless. Then, though, I'd been numb.

Today, I was the exact opposite of numb.

I'd break my fist if I tried slamming the dashboard today.

And that was precisely what I needed to do—I needed to hit. I needed to pound. I needed to destroy.

Disconnected as I felt, somewhere a code of logic

processed. I found my phone shoved into a pocket and tried to call Jolie. When it went straight to voicemail, I dialed again. This wasn't a conversation to have by phone. It was definitely not a conversation to have by voice message, but when she didn't answer the second time, I heard myself leaving a response. "You didn't tell me. How could you not. Tell. Me?"

Then I hung up and beat the phone against the dashboard until I lost my grip, and it flew out of my hand and into the back seat.

"Fuck!" I screamed into the empty car. "Fuck, fuck, fuck, fuck, fuck!"

Cursing and smashing my phone weren't helping. The storm inside me only escalated, the energy gripping me so tightly, I couldn't sit still. Rocking back and forth, I blinked the red from my eyes. Where the fuck was I?

The school was on the outskirts of Wallingford, and luckily, I'd driven away from the city rather than into it where there was no traffic on a Sunday because when I finally brought my focus to the road, I was well above the speed limit and wasn't even driving between the lines.

I moved the vehicle to the right lane, slowing down enough to realize I was near the reservoir, which was by a gun range. Maybe that was what had given me a course of action—the sign inviting me to practice my shooting. The reminder that I had Donovan's semiautomatic with me.

I pulled into the range's parking lot, hit the button to open the trunk, and left the car running when I climbed out. The gun was where I'd stashed it on Friday night, tucked into the inside pocket of my suitcase. I'd loaded the magazine when we'd arrived at Stark's house and hadn't taken it back out, which was not the way to store a gun, but it had made me sleep better in that suffocating hellhole knowing I had a loaded weapon within easy access.

Now, I tucked it into my coat pocket and closed the trunk, not bothering to zip the suitcase again. I glanced in the back window of the car as I passed on my way to the driver's seat and saw my phone lying on the floor. The screen was cracked. I wondered if it still worked.

I didn't wonder enough to find out.

If I had, maybe that would have thrown me off my current trajectory. I might have tried Jolie again and gotten her. I might have tried Donovan, who would have instantly given me a better plan. I might not have called anyone at all, but just the distraction of checking out the phone, that simple moment of pause, might have given me a chance to think. A chance to reason. A chance to acknowledge that if I got behind that wheel, there was no going back.

I didn't take that moment, and when I climbed in the front seat, I didn't hesitate at all before throwing the car into gear and peeling out of the icy lot.

Ten minutes later, I was back at the academy. As my emotions felt disconnected from my thoughts, so did my actions, and yet whatever part of me that was controlling my decisions had some sense of sanity because instead of going to the house, I found myself in the school lot.

So he won't know I'm waiting.

It was my own voice in my head and someone else's entirely.

I parked and locked the car, then set out on the mile trek to the house, careful to stay near the trees. When I got close enough, I veered off the path so I could approach from the back. As if I were a burglar daring enough to strike during daylight, my gun was pulled out and poised while I jogged hunched over until I got to the door that led into the garage. I peeked in the window.

Still only one car.

I checked my watch. It would be soon.

And as if the universe was for once working in my favor, a vehicle pulled into the driveway just then. I wouldn't have heard the garage door open after if I hadn't been listening for it, the lift was so quiet. A moment later, a car door slammed.

That quickly, he was here.

Or maybe the universe wasn't working in my favor because if I'd had to wait, I would have had time to think. Right now, I wasn't thinking at all. Not my conscious mind anyway. It was something more primitive driving me. An instinct. An impulse.

Favor or not, he was here, and reason was not.

I hugged the wall, my breaths coming fast but even, and even if I couldn't hear him inside the garage, I would have known when he passed by me. His essence inked dark and evil, and I could feel him through the layers of wood between us, shuddering through me like a ghost.

I waited until I'd heard the door to the kitchen close.

Counted to a slow ten.

Then tried the door to the garage.

It had rarely been locked during the day when I'd lived there, and it wasn't now. The kitchen door was never locked period, but it was solid with no window to peer in, and I wanted to keep the element of surprise on my side. I pressed my ear against it, listening. The sink was on. Then it turned off.

"You forgot ice," Stark said, his voice muffled but understandable.

"Ice maker's broken again," she said. "I already have a repairman coming tomorrow. I can get you some from the tray, but I know you prefer crushed."

I recognized the trepidation in her tone. She knew she would be blamed for the situation, but she was hoping she could soothe him anyway.

I hadn't forgotten that feeling. Remembering it made the hurricane of rage spin faster inside of me.

"This will be fine." His subtext said it clearly wasn't. "Fish is in the cooler. Don't leave it."

"I'll put it in the freezer now." Frantically, I looked for a place to hide, afraid he'd left the cooler in the car, but then she said, "You caught some big ones this time."

He grunted, unsatisfied with the praise.

"The weather's so good, I'm surprised you came back so early in the day. I figured you'd want to get in more time at the hole."

"There's a game at noon." College hockey, no doubt. He'd always enjoyed watching "young men duke it out." All the anger and aggression in the game, it was a sport made for him. "I wanted to be sure I was back in time."

"I'll make fried chicken then."

His voice was closer, and if she was across the room putting fish in the freezer, his back would be to me.

Again, it was instinctual. The thoughts didn't come fully formed. I just knew their likely arrangement, knew how they'd be standing when I quietly pushed the door open. Wasn't surprised to find I was right.

"Potato salad too," he demanded as I crept up behind him.

"Red potatoes okay?" When she turned back from the freezer, she saw me. There was no doubt. Our eyes met.

But though her brow wrinkled slightly, she didn't say anything until I had the gun out and pushed to the side of Stark's head. "Give me one good reason not to blow your brains out right this minute."

"Cade." My mother didn't sound at all surprised. It wasn't even an admonishment. The only emotion that I might have detected in her single word was relief.

I ignored her, lasering my attention on the man in front of me and repeated myself, slower this time. "One. Good. Reason."

His body had gone stiff, as any reasonable man's body would when the barrel of cold metal was pressed at his temple, but he played it cool. "So the prodigal son returns."

I wondered if he would have recognized my voice if my mother hadn't said my name. Wondered who else he might have thought was coming to get their reckoning. I'd always thought it had just been me and Jolie who deserved the gun-pointing kind of wrath. Then I'd learned that he'd been selling teenagers, and I'd realized there were plenty of others who would want to be in my position now.

Still, despite all the sins that he'd surely committed against countless others, all I cared about were the things he'd done to Jolie. The horrific, unspeakable, heartless things.

I was glad it was me here. Me with the weapon. Me who would make him pay.

I suddenly felt like this was what I'd been born for. This was the reason fate had brought me into the Stark household, into Jolie's life, and I was electric with the responsibility placed in my hands.

"Mind if I turn around?" he asked.

It pissed me off because I should have had him turn around already so I could keep an eye on his hands. Now if I let him, I'd be giving him power, and I refused to give him even a drop of it. "No. Hands up, and then don't move."

To his credit, he did as I said, and I actually thought he was taking me seriously for a moment.

Until he spoke again. "Call the police, Carla."

"Leave her out of it," I said.

"He won't shoot his own mother, and he's too smart to shoot me. Call them."

He was talking directly to her, so I did too this time. "You pick up the phone, and I'll kill him, Mom, so help me God."

She looked from me to him, to the gun, and back to me. Without saying a word, she turned and left the kitchen.

Shit.

For the first time since I'd left the house more than half an hour ago, I became aware of myself. Became conscious of thought. Became more than just blinding emotion.

I had a gun pointed to my stepfather's head, and my mother was likely calling the police.

What the fuck was I doing?

Fuck, fuck, fuck!

"Keep your hands up and walk." I was improvising. With the gun still at his temple, I put my other hand on his shoulder to guide him through the kitchen door into the dining room.

My mother wasn't there. Wherever she'd gone, it wasn't within sight. The smartest idea was to follow after her and be sure she didn't make any phone calls.

But none of this was smart, and when focused on that

feeling I'd had of being fated for this, I knew exactly what I was doing. And that meant I didn't care if Carla called the cops. I just needed to be sure I did what I meant to do before they got to me.

I thought quickly.

The living room and Stark's office had windows open to the front. If the police came, I'd see them in time to act. The former had too many access points. His office was more contained. Since it had always been a place of torture, there was irony doing this there. I steered him in that direction.

I'd forgotten that the door would be locked when we got there.

"The key's in my pocket," he offered. He started to lower his hand.

"Keep your fucking hands up." I didn't trust him. I pushed the gun so hard against his skull that his head leaned to the side, reminding him who was in control.

His hands went back up.

"Which pocket?" I asked.

"Left coat."

I dropped my hand from his shoulder, stuck my hand in his pocket, and found his key ring. After making sure there wasn't a Swiss Army knife or anything on them, I handed them over. "Unlock the door, then drop the keys on the ground."

Collected as he seemed, I realized it was at least somewhat of a ruse because his hand shook as he fit the key in the lock.

Not that brave after all.

That was satisfying. And not altogether shocking. In my experience, the biggest bullies were usually the most terrified when they were bullied in return. A sick glee surged through me. How far could I take this? Could I make him beg? Could I make him cry? If he shit his pants, I'd be overjoyed.

I'd never felt so delighted about the prospect of hurting someone else. Was this what it felt like to be him?

A dissonance rang in my body. I wouldn't become him. And he had to suffer. Both were true, and I didn't know if they could coexist because I would take pleasure in making him suffer, and that was the very definition of becoming him.

What the fuck am I doing?

Back to that, it seemed.

One thought at a time.

"Open the door slowly, then hands back up, and walk in. I'm right behind you." I moved the gun so it was at the back of his head, still pressed to his skull so he wouldn't forget for a second that it was there. It was damn gratifying to realize my hand was steady as could be.

I didn't pull the door closed behind me. I liked having it open so I could hear my mother if she returned. The curtains were already open, so no one was sneaking in on me there. I'd been in here a couple of times, but the situation had been different. This time, I did a quick scan, noting the everyday objects just waiting to be turned into a weapon if given a chance. When I felt I had a proper inventory, I pushed Stark away from me then told him he could turn around.

"Keep your hands where I can see them," I warned.

He turned, flashing his hands like he was a magician trying to show there was nothing up his sleeve. That's where my attention was first—his hands—and then finally, I looked at his face for the first time in seventeen years.

He studied me as I studied him. He still had his coat on. He'd aged, of course. He didn't seem quite as tall. His hair was entirely gray now. The wrinkles in his face more prominent. Even still, he looked younger than he should. Was that some sort of magic trick of his? When he'd stripped his victims of their innocence, had it gained him his youth?

He didn't deserve to be so untouched by time, and he most certainly didn't deserve to look so smug. I felt an overwhelming desire to bring my hand with the gun down hard across his face. See how smug he looked then.

It was so fucking tempting.

I took several steps until I was right up in his face and placed the tip of the Glock under his chin. "One reason, Stark. Give me one reason why you deserve to wake up another day on this planet."

The gun moved with his throat as he swallowed. "I have a feeling you'd find it more satisfying to tell me why you think I don't."

"Don't fucking be smart with me."

"Wasn't trying to be. I know we parted badly, but it's a surprising reunion to say the least."

"You should have been scared to wake up with me putting a gun to your face every day of the last seventeen years. I should have done this sooner."

"Then do it."

I felt my finger tightening on the trigger while simultaneously, my bicep shook in restraint. *Do it. Fucking do it. Just fucking do it. For what he did to her.*

It was thinking of Jolie—not what he'd done to her, but of her face, telling me she loved me—that gave me pause.

With more strength than I knew I had, I pulled the gun down and turned it to point at him again. Then I took several steps back, keeping it pinned on him as I did. "Tell me—do you know you're evil incarnate, or do you really think you're a stand-up guy?"

He started to say something, but I could tell it was going to be another wisecrack. "The truth, asshole. Do you know what you've done to people? Do you know how you've ruined lives? Do you care at all?"

He sensibly considered before speaking. "Yes, I know that my actions have an effect on others. It's not in my nature to care."

"So you don't even feel bad? Of course, you don't." I hadn't ever believed that he felt bad for what he'd done to me, but to Jolie? I thought he'd at least pretend remorse. "Just one more reason why you shouldn't live."

He tried to shrug, like he didn't care whether he did or not, but it ended up looking more like a twitch. "It might help if you tell me what I'm on trial for."

"You know what you've done." Listing his crimes would only bring him pleasure.

"And you're planning to shoot me for it? There will be repercussions, I'm sure you realize that. Your mother is a witness. Will you kill her as well?"

I hadn't thought any of it through, obviously.

Because yes, I came back with one intention only, and it was to shoot him between the eyes. I'd wanted to watch the life fade from his body, I'd wanted to know he suffered, and I'd wanted him to know who was responsible and why.

But I'd hardly thought that far, let alone about what happened after.

I'd go to jail for Jolie. I would. I'd serve the time without blinking an eye.

But I couldn't stop remembering her in my arms the night

before. The promises we'd made. Promises to be together and to never let her go, and if I killed her father...

Fuck.

There was no way Carla wouldn't turn me in. Would I ask Jolie to live a life on the run?

Stark had to see the battle in my eyes. "It's not too late to change your mind. Walk away now. I'll give you my word not to say anything."

"Like your word means anything."

"So it would be your word against mine. If you left before the police showed up, there would be little to press charges on."

He was trying to manipulate the situation, and I wanted to shoot him in the teeth for that alone. "Shut up for a minute. Just...shut up."

He was going to go down anyway. The FBI had him under investigation. He was already going to be destroyed. I really could walk away.

Would that be enough? Would he suffer enough?

"YOU DON'T HAVE A PLAN." The conceit had returned to his expression. "Which means you came here on impulse. What triggered you, I wonder."

"I said shut the fuck up!" I was in his face again, my hand on his throat, the gun at his temple. I'd lost control, if I'd ever had it in the first place. I wanted to shoot so badly I could already feel the kickback from the gun. Jolie had wanted him dead when she'd sought me out. If I'd known what he'd done to her, I would have agreed. I should shoot him right now and get it over with.

"How could you do that to her?" My hand squeezed at his

throat. "Rape your own child. Get her pregnant. I should shoot your dick off, that's what I should do. Let you bleed out from it. That's what you deserve."

"Ah. You found out about Tate." He sounded more relaxed than he had, which was the only indicator that he hadn't been relaxed before, and that made me all the more eager to inflict the pain I'd offered.

"Yeah. I found out, you bastard. Did you get off on hurting him too?" I tasted bile in the back of my throat. Jol said she'd left because he'd hit him, and while I could barely stand to think about the possibility, it occurred to me now that it could have been more. "Did you rape your son like you raped your daughter?"

"Of course not. What I had with Julianna was special." I squeezed harder at that, and his next words came out more like a rasp. "Besides, Tate isn't my son."

I let go of his throat, only to strike him across the face with the gun. "You're trying to mess with me. That's not helping you any."

His nose cracked loud and began to bleed. "No, it's the truth."

"I already told you I don't believe a word you say." This time, I pressed the tip of the gun up to his eyeball.

"Fine, don't believe me," he spat. "But I had a vasectomy. The boy is yours."

I wouldn't fall for his lies. This was his specialty—the mind-fuck. He knew exactly where a hit would land, and I would not give him that satisfaction. "She told me he wasn't, and I'm sure as hell not going to trust you over her."

"She told you that because that's what she thinks. I'm the one who told her that, and she believed it."

My hand was back at his throat. I didn't believe him for a second, and yet I couldn't stop myself from asking.

"It was the only way I could guarantee she wouldn't go running after you," he continued despite struggling to breathe. "I asked for two reports. One had Carla's swab. The other had a swab from some woman I paid on the street. I have the proof."

His face was starting to look blue. I squeezed harder. Harder.

Then I dropped my hand and stepped back.

"Where is this supposed proof?" I hated myself for falling for his trick. It was a terrible trick at that because he hadn't denied raping his daughter, just fathering Tate. Langdon Stark still needed to die.

But like I said, he knew where to throw the punch.

And this punch hurt.

Stark rubbed at his neck and did a good job at not appearing to be gasping for air while doing just that. He gestured behind him. "In the desk. Key's on the same ring as the door."

So this was the trick. Get me digging in the files, distracted, so he could overcome me or escape.

Without taking my eyes off him, I backed up to grab the keys off the floor. Then I brought them to him. "Get it."

He hesitated, calculating, maybe. Or still just trying to breathe.

After a moment, he took the keys.

He circled behind the desk and dropped in his chair. Just as he bent over, it occurred to me that I'd only looked in the locked drawer on the bottom left. I hadn't opened the bottom right, which meant I didn't know what he kept in there. I knew he had a gun in his bedroom nightstand. For all I knew, he had one there too.

"Wait. Which drawer is it in?"

He looked at me strangely. "Bottom drawer."

"Which side?"

"Left."

The keys had been in the front. Behind it had been hanging files that I hadn't looked through. There definitely hadn't been a weapon. "Okay. Go ahead."

I watched him as he bent down and jiggled with the lock. It clicked, and he slid the drawer open then flipped for several seconds through files.

"Hurry up, Stark. You're stalling."

He glared at me then pulled a folder out and dropped it on the desk. "It should be in here."

He sifted through the pages, and while it still wasn't quick enough for my taste, at least I could watch him do it now. "Here," he said eventually. He turned the report around to face me and handed it over.

I snapped it out of his hand but scanned it cautiously, keeping my gun trained on him. There was a lab logo at the top corner—ScienceLife—followed by Julianna's name and address. Then in the center of the next line, the words **Paternity Test**.

I threw my gaze back to Stark. He hadn't moved.

Back to the report. It listed two swabs had been collected—one from Tate, one from his suspected grandmother. I skimmed to the end.

Based on our analysis, it is practically proven HNDS1987656, the Alleged Paternal Grandmother, is related to the child, HNDS1987519.

My chest felt like it was yawning. Like something inside me was opening up and reaching out toward the possibility of something that should have been impossible. Something I was too scared to imagine was true.

I shook my head. "How do I know this one isn't the fake?"

"It's much easier to get a report that says negative than one that says positive. You think I've been sitting here with it in my drawer all these years just in case you came in with a gun and demanded to have proof?"

I shook my head again. He couldn't be that cruel. "If you really had a vasectomy, why get a test at all?"

He sighed impatiently. "Because vasectomies aren't one hundred percent, and I wanted to know if she'd been fucking anyone else."

"She hadn't been." I knew that as sure as I knew anything.

"If she was, they didn't get her knocked up."

I stared at the report again, wanting to read every single word in search of the flaw, but my eyes were too blurry to see anything. If he wanted to hurt me, this was the way. Convince me it was true and then tell me it was all a trick.

Actually, he wouldn't even have to do that. It hurt just as much if it was the truth. Tate was practically grown. If he was my son—we'd get a test to be sure, but something had lodged itself in that opening in my chest, something that said he was and refused to budge—then Stark had stolen his entire childhood from me. I'd missed everything. And he'd taken from my son the exact thing I'd yearned for in my own life: a father.

The rage burned hotter than ever within me, but now it was shrouded with a thick cloud of grief.

A sound I didn't recognize fell from my mouth. Something between a gasp and a sob. "Is it really true?"

But I'd taken my eye off Stark for too long, and while I'd been distracted, he must have opened the other drawer, or he'd gotten into some other secret hiding place because now when I looked at him, he was the one pointing a pistol at me.

I felt the blood rush from my face.

Then the sound of a gunshot cracked through the air.

EIGHTEEN
JOLIE

I moved the curtain back so I could see out the living room window. The street looked just as quiet as it had when I'd looked out five minutes ago. As if the view might be different twenty feet away, I crossed to the dining room window and peeked out there. This time, I saw car lights coming down the street, and I stretched my neck to get a better view of the vehicle.

It was a suburban.

Not the rental car that Cade and I had picked up.

Biting my lip, I let the curtain fall and crossed back to the front door to make sure the porch lights were on.

"You're making me anxious," Tate said.

I turned toward him and blinked until my own anxious thoughts parted long enough to register him. His textbooks were spread across the dining room table, his headphones wrapped around his neck, a bag of Lay's Cheddar & Sour

Cream Flavored Potato Chips open in front of him. He reached in and brought out a handful of chips.

"Why are you snacking before dinner?" I marched over and grabbed the bag and moved it to the kitchen so he couldn't eat more.

"Because it's seven o'clock, and you haven't started cooking anything."

Was it really already seven? We'd arrived home just before noon, and I'd expected Cade to show up soon after. When he was still MIA at two, I had my first doubts—was he not coming? Was this his revenge? Him bailing on me this time?

It was Tate who reminded me I'd turned my phone off during the drive, and I brightened considerably when I saw a voice message waiting from Cade.

Until I listened to the message.

Ever since then, I'd had a lump in my throat and a bowling ball in my stomach and a sense of foreboding that increased a degree every time I replayed the message—which had been plenty—even though I'd immediately memorized both the words and Cade's gut-torn cadence. *You didn't tell me. How could you not. Tell. Me?*

There was only one secret I was still keeping from him. A secret I'd tried to tell him last night. He couldn't have found out on his own, could he? But what else could he mean?

And as each quarter hour passed without word from him, years of shame felt validated. Who would want a woman who'd been raped by her father? Who would want a woman who loved and raised a child born from that abuse?

My greatest fear, and the one that had kept me from telling him, was that Cade would think differently about me once he knew. I'd known rationally that it was a silly worry, especially back then when we were both under my father's thumb. Part of me even thought he already knew. At times, it had seemed like it couldn't be more obvious—the way my father treated me. How he locked me up. How he did a bedroom check on me at least once a night. I'd thought Cade had figured it all out and that he hadn't cared.

Wishful thinking on my part.

I'd hoped he'd known, but deep down, I knew he didn't. And I hadn't told him myself because I was ashamed. Because I was afraid it would matter to him. Plus, keeping it secret made it easier to pretend it wasn't happening. I'd dealt with it for so long that I'd learned how to tuck it away from my reality. Once I said it aloud, it would have to come out of the dark, and that would make it real.

And it was the worst real thing.

"Mom?"

I shook my head out of the shame spiral and tried to remember what we'd been talking about. "You could make dinner yourself, you know."

I immediately regretted snapping. "I'm sorry." I crossed over to him and gave him a hug. "I'll order Panda to make up for it."

He tried to shrug me off, but I wouldn't let go. "It's fine. Panda's good. I don't need the hug."

"The hug is for me." I hugged him tighter.

With a sigh, he put his hand over my arm. "Maybe he had car trouble. And his phone died. Or he decided to stay with his mom longer."

"Maybe. Maybe."

"He wouldn't have talked to me about being in our lives if he was going to ditch us."

"Yeah. Right. I'm not worried."

He was kind enough not to address my blatant lie. I was out-of-my-skull worried. Barring a horrible accident—and God, that would really be horrible—there was no plausible excuse for his absence, and we both knew it. If he'd had car trouble, he would have called. If his phone had died, enough time had passed for him to have charged it. If he'd decided to stay longer at the house, he would have seen my father.

This was the excuse I couldn't stop thinking about because it was the worst of the bunch and also somehow the most likely. Even more likely, I imagined, than Cade having second thoughts about us. Especially after the message he'd left because if he meant what I thought he meant, who could have told him except Dad?

If they'd had an encounter, I almost hoped that Cade had been too grossed out by the truth and that was the reason he wasn't here now. It was better than the alternative—that my father had prevented him from coming.

I couldn't let myself think about that.

Realizing I was squeezing my child probably a little too hard, or at least harder than he would have liked, I let him go and returned once again to the window. Then I pulled out my phone and made sure it was still on. That the ringer was up. That I had no messages. I called his number. It went instantly to voicemail. I hung up and tucked the phone back into my pocket.

"Mom?" he said impatiently. As if I'd forgotten something.

But when I replayed our last words, the conversation seemed to have stopped in a natural place. I drew my brows together in question.

"Do you want *me* to order Panda?"

Ah, right. Dinner. "Yes. Sorry. I'm...Please. Do."

He pulled his laptop closer and started typing. "What do you want me to order for you?"

"Nothing. Anything." I wasn't hungry.

I crossed back to the living room window.

"Should I get extra in case Cade—?"

"Yes." I wasn't going to lose hope. I refused. "He'll be here."

Then, as if declaring it out loud had summoned him, my phone rang.

I answered before there was a chance for a second ring. "Oh, my God, where are you? Are you okay? Is everything okay?"

"Jol?" He sounded exhausted, and that mattered, but it was better than not hearing a sound from him at all.

"I'm here." I tried not to speak so quickly this time but didn't do well at succeeding. "Where are you? Did you get lost? Are you...okay?"

"No." He cleared his throat. "I'm not lost, I mean. I'm sorry, babe. You must have been worried."

"Yes, I've been worried!" I could feel Tate's eyes on me, and I turned to him. "I expected you hours ago. What happened?"

Tate made a gesture that said, *Well?*

I gave him one back that said, *I don't know.*

"I'd really rather talk to you in person." Cade didn't just sound exhausted—he sounded run over. "I just wanted to call now that I had a chance. I, um. My phone broke."

He had more to say, but all the nervous energy inside of me pushed me to interrupt. "Your phone *broke*? How did it break?"

He tried to chuckle. "I might have beaten it against the dash a few times."

"You...what?"

"Listen, I'll tell you everything when I get there. I would have called sooner, but the broken phone thing, and I didn't have your number or your address anywhere but on my cell—trust me, I've memorized them now—so I had to stop in Hartford and get a new one."

"Hartford? You're in Hartford now?" He was giving me information, but it wasn't enough or it wasn't connecting. I still felt as confused as I'd been before I answered. "But you're still coming?"

"I'm headed to you now."

"Okay, good. That's good." I did the math. "You'll be here about nine then."

"Yeah. I will." I heard the car turn on then, and I pictured him sitting in the parking lot of the phone store, calling me before he got back on the road.

But Hartford was only twenty minutes from Wallingford. Where had he been for the eight hours before that?

He'd said he'd beaten his phone against the dash. It had to be connected to his earlier call. *You didn't tell me. How could you not. Tell. Me?*

"Cade...the message you left..."

"I'll explain everything when I get there, Jol."

I didn't know if I could take another ninety minutes plus of anguish. But he'd called. And he was coming. And I trusted him. "Okay. See you soon."

CADE MUST HAVE SPED because he pulled into my driveway less than ninety minutes later. The kitchen window looked out on that side of the house, so I pretended to do dishes and sneakily watched him get out of the car, stretch, then look from the side door to the front of the house, as if not sure which to use.

When I felt his eyes move toward me, I made sure to lower mine. As anxious as I'd been for him to arrive, I was also nervous about him being here. I was pretty sure I would have been nervous if he'd shown up when he was supposed to. It was one thing to cling to each other when we were surrounded by memories of the past. It was quite another to bring him into my present.

Now he was showing up late. Add to that his mysterious voice message and evasive phone call, and I felt unmoored.

He ended up choosing the front door, and as I opened it and invited him in, I regretted not running out the side door to greet him as soon as he'd driven in. Greeting him here was too formal. Like he was a guest coming to our house rather than a man who was coming home, and of course, that's what he was—a guest—but it wasn't how I wanted him to feel.

It wasn't how I wanted to feel about him.

The awkwardness could have been fixed with an embrace, but I couldn't bring myself to take the step toward him. There was a wall around him, thick and impenetrable, and instead of feeling natural with him like I had in the early morning hours in his arms, I felt like I had when I'd arrived at his office in New York more than a week ago.

It didn't help that he hadn't brought his suitcase from the car.

All of a sudden, I wanted to cry.

I feigned cheerfulness instead. "You found us all right?"

"Yep." He shut the door behind him and scanned his surroundings.

I tried to see it from his eyes. The hotel we'd stayed in this past week had been bigger than my main floor. The furniture nicer, too. My fifteen-hundred-square-foot HUD home looked shabby in comparison.

"It's small." It was an apology.

"It's nice."

"Not what you're used to, I'm sure."

"I love it." He was too polite. He was too distant. "What I can see of it."

"Oh. You want a tour?" It would take two minutes to show him the whole house.

"How about later?"

"Yeah, later's good.

It wasn't really my home I was ashamed of. He knew what it was like to be dirt poor, and we were much better off than that. He had money now, but I knew he wasn't materialistic.

The shame came from somewhere else, from the thing I thought he knew. That was the thing with shame though—it grew like ragweed, rapidly spreading from only a small seedling. It wouldn't have mattered if I was inviting Cade into my twenty-million-dollar mansion. I would have still felt unattractive, out of place, and a pest.

But maybe I was jumping to conclusions, and he really didn't know, and I was freaking out for nothing. "Are you hungry? We ordered Chinese. Not good Chinese. The franchised kind. We didn't know what you'd like, so we have a bit of everything."

"Thank you. I picked up something on the road. I'm sorry."

"No, no worries. Now we have an easy dinner for tomorrow." I tried to laugh, but it didn't sound natural. He was definitely acting weird, and I was definitely acting weird, and in my heart of hearts, I knew that something was very, very wrong.

I could feel rather than hear Tate coming up behind me. His presence was confirmed when Cade lifted his chin in his direction. "Hey."

"Hey," Tate said back.

"Homework?"

"Taking a break."

He studied Tate for a long moment. Too long, and I knew then, knew without a doubt, that Cade had found out. He was looking at him with new eyes. Trying to see any defects that children born of incest sometimes display. I, too, had looked for those traits over the years. It was natural when I did it.

I didn't like someone else looking at him like that. Not even Cade.

Irritated about that and about the tension between us and about feeling less than and about the hours he'd kept me waiting and about the answers I'd yet to receive, I decided I was done with the bullshit small talk. "What the fuck happened today?"

If Cade was surprised by my directness, he didn't show it. He glanced again at Tate. "Do you want to talk alone?"

"No." Talking alone was never good. "Tate's been anxiously waiting for an explanation as well. He deserves to hear it."

Cade didn't argue. "Why don't we sit down?"

"I don't want to fucking sit down. I want you to stop fucking stalling and tell me what the fuck's going on." Not being prone to cursing or outbursts, the two used in combo tended to do an excellent job of getting people's attention.

In turn, he got to the point. "Your father is dead."

"Wha?"

It was more of a sound than a word, but he understood enough to repeat himself. "Your father. Langdon. He's dead."

"He's...? For sure?"

"For sure."

The air was suddenly thin.

Or absent.

I was stunned.

Or relieved.

Or sad?

My heart thundered for a few erratic beats. "I think I should sit down."

I felt disconnected from my feet as they took me into the living room. When I sank down on the sofa, Tate was suddenly at my side, his arm around my back. "Mom? Are you okay?"

Cade was there too, kneeling in front of me like he was about to propose, and though I didn't feel him taking my hand, he was holding it in his when I looked down. I watched him rub his thumb across my knuckles, and I thought, *that feels good.*

And I thought, *this is why he's acting weird.*

And I thought, *I should have dusted the floor.*

And I thought, *my father's dead.*

"I don't know how to feel." I was skipping ahead. "How?"

Cade didn't take his eyes off of mine. "Gunshot wound."

Someone had a vise grip around my torso, and it tightened around me. "You?"

He hesitated, and again, I couldn't breathe.

"No," he said finally.

The grip on my chest loosened. Slightly.

"I wanted to," he continued. "I would have. I went there

planning..." He glanced at Tate and seemed to regret what he'd been about to admit.

"From what I hear, he deserved it," Tate said.

That encouraged Cade. "He did. I'm not ashamed to say I don't feel bad about it at all."

"Don't you dare feel bad about it." My vision was swimming. I brought my hand up to my cheek and found it was wet. Which was confusing because I'd wanted my father dead. Truly.

So why was my eye leaking?

I ignored it. "You saw him? You saw it happen? What happened?"

"I left soon after you did. But I went back." Cade gestured something to Tate.

Tate's arm left my shoulder so he could reach over to grab a Kleenex from the box on the side table. Then he thought better of it and grabbed the whole box.

I took one, but my attention was pinned on Cade. "You went back?"

"I did. I..." He hesitated long enough for me to know he was leaving something out. "I wanted to make him pay. For everything. Everything he's done to...us. And I meant to do it, Jol. I was going to make him suffer. But then he pulled out his own gun and pointed it at me."

The vise grip tightened again.

"And then Carla shot him," he said.

"Carla?" The shock momentarily stopped the tears.

"She came in behind me. I didn't have any idea she was there. She must have grabbed the gun that you'd said was in the bedroom, and when your father pointed his gun at me, I thought I was dead. I swear I saw my life flash before my eyes.

When the gun went off, I actually looked down, looking for the wound. I thought it had been me because it wasn't my gun that had gone off.

"But then I saw your father. A shot right between the eyes. He fell over his desk, and when I looked behind me, there was Carla, holding a pistol with both hands wrapped around it."

"Carla," I said again. Because it was easier to think about that part than the part where Cade had almost been dead. "Carla shot him."

"I was surprised too. Who would have predicted?" He was trying to hide his emotion, but I heard it now. All the years that Carla had stood by while her husband had abused her son... Cade had never believed his mother cared about him at all. It had to have an impact on him.

My hands flew to cup his face. "Oh, Cade."

He brought one of his hands to cover one of mine. "I'm fine."

He couldn't be. He'd been upset enough to confront my father—upset enough to want to kill him in cold blood—and then my father had pulled a gun on him...

The tears turned into full-blown sobs.

Obviously, I was *not* fine.

"I'm so sorry, Mom." Tate patted me in that way he did whenever I got emotional, and I'd already broken down once on him today. Poor guy didn't always know how to react when I showed vulnerability.

Cade, however, did.

He sat up so he could wrap his arms around me. I clutched onto his shirt and cried on his shoulder while he rubbed his hand soothingly on my back.

"He. Had. A. Gun. Pointed. At you," I said, stuttering

through sobs. It wasn't the only reason I was crying, but it was the easiest to explain, even to myself. "You could be dead. It could have been you."

"I'm not, though." He kissed my hair, then hugged me tighter. "And he is."

"And he was so awful."

"Yes, he was."

"Then why am I sad?"

"Oh, baby." He rocked me back and forth. "He was your father, and now he's dead, and every possibility of him being something better or different to you is gone."

"Yeah." That was probably it.

"And you loved him."

"I think I sort of did."

"Of course you did. And that's okay."

I'd thought my tears were slowing, but another wave crashed over me. It was complicated, all the things I was feeling. They rolled together into a muddy mess. I wasn't entirely sure that I wasn't crying partly in celebration.

A large part of it was definitely relief.

Relief that my father was dead, and Cade was alive. Relief that he was here, holding me.

Relief knowing that whatever came between us from here on out, it would no longer be Langdon Stark.

The cage door was open, and this bird was finally free.

NINETEEN
JOLIE

Fortunately, the crying didn't last too long, though it left me weary and with a headache. Tate still had homework, but he made me a cup of tea before retreating to finish it in the basement. He'd adopted the extra room down there at the start of the school year, abandoning the bedroom upstairs next to mine for his own space.

Once he'd gone, Cade had insisted I take a bath. He drew it up for me using generous amounts of the cherry-blossom bath salts I kept on the shelf, then helped undress me and get settled. I'd been disappointed when he hadn't joined me, but once I was alone in the steamy room with a washcloth on my forehead, I appreciated the privacy.

I would need a lot of these moments, I realized, before I fully processed everything that had happened with my father.

Not just today, but over the course of the rest of my life. I'd done work in therapy to deal with a lot of it, but he wasn't like a tree that I could hack off and be done with. He was seeded into me, a stubborn weed that mingled with other growth, sprouting when better parts of my life were in full bloom. I would dig him out at the root then, but that didn't mean he wouldn't return again and again and again.

This time, when I hacked at the plant, I'd manage even better because Cade would be next to me. Right?

He said he would. I had to believe that he still meant it.

By the time the water was cold and my fingers were pruned, I figured I'd done enough weeding for the night. I climbed out, toweled off, and put on the white fluffy bathrobe that Cade must have found in my closet and laid out on the counter for me.

I wasn't sure what I'd been expecting when I came out, but when I opened the bathroom door, I had to lean against the frame because the sight in front of me made me dizzy.

"You look good on my bed," I said. He was stretched out on top of the covers, his phone in his hand, and he didn't just look good—he looked divine. It helped that he wasn't wearing anything but his black jeans. Something about seeing him barefoot as well as shirtless did extraordinary things to the space between my legs.

It was strange to acknowledge sexual thoughts after an evening spent dealing with Dad, but that had frequently been my way of coping. He'd ingrained a desire to please. Taught me that was the way to receive love. It took work to separate the real from what he'd programmed. Was sex what I really wanted right now? Or was it enough that Cade was here?

It would have been enough if I knew he was *really* here, and I was too scared/tired/unsure to find out, so yes, sex would substitute nicely.

He'd been focused on whatever he was reading and must

not have heard the door open because he looked up in surprise at the sound of my voice. Avoiding my comment, he set his cell down on the nightstand and swung his legs over the side of the bed. "How are you feeling?"

"I could be feeling better. You could make me feel better."

His eyes darkened as they swept over my body, but he followed with the words I'd been wanting to put off. "We should talk."

I wondered if I could convince him to put it off.

But I'd promised him I'd tell him. Since he'd found out before I'd had the chance, I couldn't let him wait longer for that discussion. He deserved this.

And his shirt was off, and his suitcase was leaning against the wall, so he planned to stay for at least tonight.

"Okay."

He didn't start, though, and knowing where to start myself was daunting.

Well, if I got to choose, I'd start where I wanted to. "Your message. You asked why I hadn't told you..." I swallowed. "How did you find out?"

"Carla guessed."

I let out a sound that was half *ha* and half *huh*. Decades too late, but good for her.

I wanted to care how she'd felt about it.

No, actually, I didn't even want to care. I wanted to want to, but I didn't. I only cared about Cade. "That was why you broke your phone. And why you went back to the house. With a gun."

"I..." He took a breath in. Let it out. "Reacted."

He didn't add *poorly*. Most people would expect that word to follow.

Most people didn't understand what we'd dealt with.

He'd reacted *naturally*, as far as I was concerned. I'd wanted to kill my father as well.

Still, it was moving. That Cade had reacted like that. That he'd been upset enough to want to kill the man who'd hurt me. It affected me deeply, but it didn't tell me everything I needed to know. Just because he'd been angry enough to kill didn't mean everything was okay between us. Was I the same person in his eyes knowing what he knew now? Was Tate?

There was definitely something that had changed. Something he had yet to say that he hadn't. "Go ahead," I coaxed. "Say what you need to say. I'm ready." I wasn't ready.

He let out a slow breath. "I understand why you didn't tell me. I shouldn't have inferred that I didn't."

I hadn't seen that coming. "Because it's a terrible thing, and you'd rather not know?"

"Because it's a very terrible thing, and I'd rather it hadn't happened. And I wish I had known. I wish to God that I had known."

"Because it changes how you think of me?"

"No." He jerked like I'd slapped him. "No."

"Why then? Do you think there was something you could have done to stop it?" It came out harsh. A judgment.

I expected him to be defensive.

Instead, he responded honestly. "I'd like to think I would have tried. But I hadn't tried to stop any of it."

"Exactly." I didn't add that it would have gotten him killed because I was being an asshole. Everything was coming out mean, and I felt shitty about it, but I couldn't stop myself. It was like I was so afraid he was going to hurt me that I kept trying to hurt him first.

He understood that. Somehow. And he didn't let my bullets land.

He didn't let me shoot again, either, because he stood up and crossed to me. When he put his hands on my waist, I was disarmed. "I wish I'd known, Jol, so that you could have leaned on me. I wish I'd known so you wouldn't have had to carry it alone. I could have done that for you."

My lip quivered. "I didn't want you to have to carry any of it."

"I get it." One hand swept the damp ends of my hair off my shoulder and rested on my neck, and I liked feeling held, but I also felt vulnerable because I didn't believe he did get it. He *couldn't* get it. How could he? I barely got it, and it had happened to me.

It was like he could read my thoughts because he used his thumb to tilt my chin up, and he said, "I promise I get it, Jolie. Because I didn't tell you either."

Now I didn't get him.

And then I did, and my stomach dropped. "You... What did he do?"

"Nothing compared to what he did to you. It only happened once. Near the end. I'd cried—I usually didn't—and I guess that...aroused him. The beating stopped, and when I got brave enough to look behind me, he was...taking care of himself."

"Cade!" My arms dropped, and I brought my palms to his chest. The horror made me forget about protecting myself, and I only cared about protecting him.

He covered one of my hands with his. "Like I said, it was nothing comparatively. He didn't do anything but that. He never touched me in a sexual manner. And I was still so fucking humiliated by it. I couldn't bear for you to find out."

"Yes." Oh, my God, yes.

"I wouldn't have even known how to say it."

"That's exactly it. And I thought you'd blame me."

His eyes met mine for the first time since his admission. "I would never have blamed you for that. *Never*."

"I know. I really do. It's stupid when I say it, but I felt it. I worried you'd think I was *too* broken. That you wouldn't want to touch me, knowing I wasn't just yours."

He cupped my face. "Baby, you were always just mine, no matter what he did to you. He stole that. It wasn't his to take. And if I'd known, I would have touched you more. I would have tried to erase every memory of his touch from your body."

"You did. You did that without even knowing."

"I wish I'd done more. I wish I'd stolen you away from there."

"I was pregnant. The odds of Tate having a severe defect were fifty percent. We couldn't have handled that on our own. Without money? Without support? It wasn't a risk I could take."

"I need to—"

But I wasn't done, and this was important, so I cut him off. "By the time I knew he was okay, you were long gone. And even if I'd found you, I didn't know that you could love me after... I didn't know that you could love *him*."

He knew that what I was really saying was, *Can you still love him?*

"About that..." He dropped his hands from my face.

No.

I took a step back. Away. Tate and I were a package deal.

He couldn't accept what my father had done to me without accepting him. Without loving him.

But Cade hadn't been pulling away. He'd only let go of me so he could take something out of his pocket—a paper, folded up into a square. No, two papers, I realized as he unfolded it. A familiar logo at the top caught my eye.

I'd seen that report already. It was burned in my memory and then burned in the fire. How did he have a copy? Did he think I didn't know?

He held it out toward me. "Your father showed me this."

"I've seen it."

"The one you saw was fake."

My heart did an involuntary flip before I got control of myself. "It wasn't fake. Did he try to tell you it was?"

"Maybe it wasn't. But he said he'd gotten a swab from a woman on the street for the one you saw. This report is the one that had Carla's DNA."

I was immediately angry. At my father, not at Cade. Though a little bit at Cade for being swept into whatever last game my father had tried to play. And a little less mad than I'd ever been at Carla for making sure he couldn't play any games again. "He was lying to you."

But I took the report from his hands because I was also gullible where my father was concerned and because I was as desperate to believe another truth as Cade was.

"You're right. He could have been lying," he said as I read. "I acknowledge that. But he said he'd had a vasectomy. Did you know that?"

I didn't. Could that really be true?

"He made me take all those damn pregnancy tests." I was

skimming the text as I had back then. Seeing a different outcome this time—an outcome I really wanted to believe.

Had my father known every time that those tests would come back negative? Why *had* they? He'd been raping me since I was thirteen. Cade was the only other man I'd let inside me.

"And that last night we were together?" There was a thread of excitement in Cade's voice now, just barely there, as if he was trying to contain it. "I'd thrown my jeans on, but the condom was broken when I finally got a chance to dispose of it."

"It was broken?"

"I'd figured it had torn in my escape, but it could have been torn before."

It would have been the right timing. Even if it hadn't been that night, there had been other times we'd been less than careful.

"And Tate has my earlobes. I noticed tonight. Your lobes attach to your head at the bottom. So did your father's. Not Tate's."

I looked at the sides of Cade's head and saw ears that I'd seen every day for almost seventeen years. I couldn't remember what my mother's ears had been like. Had they been attached?

"I love him no matter what, Jol." Now he was definitely excited. And sincere. "We can get another DNA test, if you want, but he's mine. I don't need a test to know it."

Honestly?

I didn't need a test either.

I already knew. I'd always known. I'd always seen Cade in my son and had excused it as seeing what I'd wanted to see, but I'd also somehow known. It was partly why I'd told Tate that Cade was his father in the first place. Not just because I'd wanted that but because I'd *known*. The only reason I hadn't ever gotten a second test was because I'd been afraid that finding out that what I knew to be true was wrong would have destroyed me.

Now my father was dead, and Cade was standing in front of me, claiming my son as his. I could question the report in my hand, say we needed to verify it, and give my father another chance to take this moment from us too.

Or I could accept what I'd always known as truth.

"He's yours," I said. Relieved. Joyful. Exhilarated. "We don't need a test. He's yours."

His grin reached his eyes. "He's ours."

"He really is—"

And then it hit me in full.

What this meant.

What I'd done.

"Oh, Cade." My legs couldn't support me anymore. He tried to catch me on my way down but only managed to hold on to my arms as he came with me to the ground. This time, my sobs came without tears, shuddering through my body like mini earthquakes. "Cade. I kept him from you. You missed so much. You missed everything."

This shame felt entirely different from the humiliation that came from my father's assault. That shame focused on myself. This shame came from outside of me, came from recognizing what I'd done to someone I loved very much. Two someones. This shame was majority guilt, and the pain of it was like none I'd ever known.

"Baby." We were both on our knees, and he tried to pull me into his arms, tried to comfort me.

I couldn't let him.

I braced my hands on his shoulders to keep him from me. "Don't you dare tell me this is okay. This is unforgivable."

"This isn't..." He closed his mouth, wisely realizing he should consider before he said anything he didn't actually mean.

I knew what I meant already and didn't have to think about it. "You can't tell me it's not. You missed your son's whole life."

"His life isn't over. It's just beginning."

"You missed him growing up. You missed years you can never get back. You will never be able to repair that completely. It's not okay."

"I know, okay? I know. Believe me, I know. I've had hours to think about it, and I know." His eyes were glossy.

That got mine flooding as well, and I clutched onto his shoulders, my nails digging involuntarily into his back. "I'm so sorry. I'm so, so sorry." I could barely get the words out.

This time, when he pulled me into him, I let him hold me, let him rock me back and forth. Let him cry with me.

When my sobs began to be less violent, I let him pull me with him to the ground so that we were lying face-to-face.

He calmed faster than I had, and he whispered soothing words that I was unable to hear and stroked my hair with more love than I'd felt in years.

When my hiccups slowed, he wiped my face with his palm and tried again. "Jolie, this is not your fault."

"It is! I could have—"

He caught my eyes with his. "This is. Not. Your. Fault. It's not. This is him. No one else. Blaming anyone but him gives him yet another win. After everything he's taken, we can't let him have this too."

"But I left him a decade ago. I should have—"

"No!" He said it so sharply, it startled me to attention. "No more regrets. We can't go back, and I don't want to. I want to go forward with you and my son." His voice cracked on the last word, and I'd never heard anything so beautiful.

Still, I couldn't let go of what he'd lost. What Tate had lost. "You don't know him. He doesn't know you."

"But I will. He will. I'm going to spend so much time with that kid, he's going to be sick of me. I'm not missing a single moment from now on."

"Not a single moment." Admittedly, I liked hearing that for selfish reasons. If he was here for Tate, he'd be here for me.

"And we'll have another baby." He tucked a piece of hair behind my ear. "I know that won't make up for what I missed, but you'll tell me. Every milestone that our baby goes through, you'll tell me what I missed with Tate."

"Okay."

I must not have sounded sure because he asked again. "Okay?"

And since it seemed he really wanted to know, I thought about it before I spoke. "It's never not going to be sad."

"No, it's not. But we can grieve together." He swept his knuckles across my jaw. "I have to tell you, Jolie—I'm sad, but also I'm so tired of life without you. Exhausted from it. There isn't any pain I can't get over as long as I can suffer it next to you."

My next breath quivered, but it was an afterquake. I was feeling calmer now. The ground solid beneath me, both literally and figuratively. "I don't think you can understand how in love with you I am."

"Don't bet on that." He stroked my skin, his touch soothing and intimate, and I let myself feel how much he loved me as his fingers explored my neck and collarbone, his eyes never leaving mine.

God, he loved me. He did, and I knew it as surely as I knew that Tate was his. He'd proven himself and beyond. "You would have killed for me."

"I would have." The depth of his love was in his sincerity. "I wanted to hurt him for hurting you."

"I think he hurt anyway because he knew I loved you more than him."

"It wasn't enough. He deserved much more pain."

"He doesn't deserve to take any more of our energy, though. Or our time. I don't want to give him any more of me. I want to give all of that to you."

"I'll take it." His face was nearer to mine than it had been. Had he moved closer, or had I?

I was just thinking I wanted more of him—all of him—when his lips found mine. His kisses were slow. Not hesitant but lingering. Between, his mouth worshiped my jaw and my neck and my throat, always returning to my lips before they had a chance to feel neglected.

It was a natural progression for his hand to slip inside my bathrobe. For his thumb to rub over my nipple and then slide between my legs where I was already swollen and waiting. It was nothing at all for him to make me come, and he swallowed my whimpers, not because we were afraid of being heard by an abusive father, but because he liked the taste of them.

He chased my cries with my pussy juice, licking his finger clean before divesting me of my robe entirely. Then, taking my hand in his, he rose from the floor, pulling me with him and over to the bed where he laid me out and feasted on me with his eyes while he took off his jeans.

Then he climbed over my body and slipped inside me, and I felt joined to him like I had that day that he'd dressed my ring finger with a pipe cleaner and asked me to be his wife, and also not at all like that day. Because that union had been fragile, and even when I'd earnestly said yes, I'd known the obstacles in our way. Then, yes had felt like a wish.

Now, yes was a promise, and I said it over and over as he thrust inside me. Yes, yes, yes. From this day forward, let us never be apart.

After, when the lights were off and the covers pulled over us, I nuzzled my face in his neck, relishing the smell of man and sex that had been absent from my room for way too long.

"I feel good about that round," he said, kissing my hair. "Those were my best swimmers."

I laughed, my nipples sharpening as my breasts brushed his chest. "I'm not as young as I once was. We might have to do that a lot."

"Oh, we're definitely doing that a lot." This kiss he planted on my lips. "Do we need to tell Tate?"

"That we're doing it a lot?"

"That we want another. Will he feel...replaced?"

There was a delicious pinch in my heart. He was instantly a good father, and I'd never been happier. "I don't think so, but we'll make sure he knows that's not the goal."

"Maybe we should save it. Let him get used to the idea that I'm in his life for good first."

"Yeah. We should tell him that part. Soon."

"That I'm his father?" He corrected himself. "That I know I'm his father? What time is it? Should we do it now?"

I laughed again, animated by his eagerness. "It's late, and if he's not asleep, he's finishing homework."

"Tomorrow."

"After school," I specified.

"After school," he agreed. "Tell me about him, will you?"

I smiled and wiped the tears that had gathered in the corners of my eyes.

Then, my fingers laced through his, I told my true love all about our son.

TWENTY
CADE

I woke up alone. The scent of bacon filled the air, though the placement of the sun said it was closer to lunch than breakfast. Since we'd stayed up talking until almost four, I wasn't surprised that I'd slept in, but I was surprised how good I felt. It was the first day since I'd seen Jolie that I hadn't woken up reaching for a cigarette.

Good thing, too, since the pack I'd bought was empty, and I'd vowed to not buy another.

I wouldn't have minded reaching for Jolie, though.

I threw my legs over the side of the bed, and while I was considering whether I wanted to take a shower before or after I found her, a buzzing came from the nightstand.

My new phone.

I hadn't bothered with the charger, and I'd expected it to be dead, but apparently, Jolie had plugged it in.

Good woman.

I wasn't used to being cared for. Most women I bedded

were usually kicked out before I went to sleep. This was different. This was fucking fantastic.

But the buzzing...

I managed to answer before it went to voicemail.

"About time you fucking answered. You leave me a message like you did yesterday and then don't take any of my calls? You're lucky I didn't drive out there myself looking for you."

Donovan didn't just sound concerned—he sounded pissed off.

"I expected you to call back last night." He'd been the second call I'd made after I'd bought the phone. I'd called him again when Jolie had been in the bath. It wasn't like him not to return a call that involved topics like guns and death and DNA tests.

"Yeah, well, I have shit of my own, you know. I don't just sit around waiting to fix your life."

Beyond pissed off. That's what he was. I could tell from its intensity that the emotion had nothing to do with me and rather was applied to everything in its way.

Which wasn't like Donovan either. He tended to be in control of everything, most notably his own emotions.

"What bug got up your ass?" I asked, but the tone was playful.

"My ass is bug-free, asshole."

"That true?"

He took a beat. "No. But that's all I'm giving you."

Had to be about Sabrina. I debated pushing him—I imagined the guy needed someone to look after him sometimes, the way he looked after everyone else.

Problem was that he wasn't prone to letting anyone in, and

no one knew how to bully their way past personal boundaries as well as he did.

I ran a hand up and down my thigh, not sure what to offer him. "Anything I can do?"

"You can shut the fuck up, and let me update you on what I know."

I stifled a laugh. I'd barely given him any details when I'd left the message for him, and of course, he knew more now than I did. That sounded about right.

"Shutting the fuck up now."

"Spoke to Leroy, my FBI guy. A big bust went down this morning, seventy men arrested in total for charges of human trafficking. It's on all the news, if you haven't looked already. Stark would have been part of that, as well as your mother. You saved the government the cost of a trial, which I'm sure someone appreciates because he most definitely would have been in cuffs today."

My breath came in sharp. "My mother?" She'd gone willingly into custody after the shooting the day before, though the detective in charge had said she'd likely be let go as soon as they investigated since it was essentially a case of defending others.

"Figured that was what you'd pick up on rather than the seventy people involved in human trafficking. This was way bigger than your douche of a stepfather. Real finessed operation. Several others involved had access to kids the way Stark did—some other private school teachers, coaches, one was a librarian. They were spread across the nation, and they rotated abductions so no one looked suspicious."

"Blamed them all on runaways," I interjected, understanding how it worked.

"Correct. The abductor would take the kid to a meetup and

be paid in cash for delivery. It's been going on for over two decades."

And Stark had been involved for probably all of it. "What happened to the kids?"

"Most were sold overseas. Imagine what you will what kind of slaves they became."

I shuddered. My skin felt like it was crawling. "They're going home now, though, right?"

Donovan's pause told me the answer before he spoke. "They've been able to locate a few that were in domestic situations. International is harder to track down, but there are a lot of people working on it. I know Edward Fasbender from Accelecom has been working with my FBI friend, Leroy, and financing rescues. You want in on that?"

"Yes. Yes, I do."

"I'll set it up for both of us. Meanwhile, this is a big takedown. The spotlight's everywhere on it. You may want to lay low. That school is going to be crawling with press."

"We're in Boston now, so I think we're good."

"You are? Good." He wasn't often surprised, and I couldn't help feeling smug that I'd managed to keep something off his radar for once. "As for your mother—are you ready for this?"

So much for feeling smug. With that lead up, I had a feeling whatever he said next was going to throw me for a loop. "I'm sitting down, if that counts."

"She's been Stark's wingman since the beginning. Before they even got married, but according to her, she was basically blackmailed into it. She says she accidentally found herself doing a favor for him while they were dating—a favor that basically threw her into the business of sex trafficking—and then he used that to keep her under his thumb for the next twenty years."

"Sounds like a likely excuse."

"Maybe that's all it is, but this isn't what she told them last night—this is what she told them a month ago. That insider giving info to the feds was no other than Carla Stark, neé Warren."

I blinked. Then ran a hand over my face. "Okay?"

"Okay? That's all you have to say about that? Dude, it's your mom."

I rolled a kink out of my shoulder, turning my head in time to see Jolie walking through the door with a tray of breakfast wearing nothing but my T-shirt.

At least, I assumed it was only the T-shirt. I'd have to do some investigating to be sure.

Whoa, I mouthed with a smile, then responded to Donovan. "I don't know what to say, Kincaid. Is that supposed to make up for all the shit she overlooked over the years? Am I supposed to think of her as just another one of Stark's victims?"

"No. You aren't supposed to think anything. Just thought you'd be more interested."

Maybe I would have been. Before Jolie and I had decided to put the past behind us and stop giving energy to the people who had hurt us. "Does this mean she's going to jail?"

"If she does, it will be a light sentence. That was her exchange for providing information willingly. Want me to keep you updated?"

I almost missed the question. Jolie had bent to lower the tray to the dresser, and I was too busy tilting my head to see if I would catch a peek of something naughty. "Uh, nah. I'm good."

"You're good," he repeated. More bewildered than questioning. "Didn't she save your life yesterday?"

"Look, D. The first time she gave me life, she fucked me over repeatedly afterward. I'm grateful she was there, and I told her as such before she left with the police, but now I'm going to cut my losses and be done with her. I told her that as well. She seemed to understand."

"Huh. That's a surprisingly grown-up attitude."

With a piece of bacon in hand, Jolie came over then and sat on my lap. She offered the piece toward me as she whispered, "Donovan?"

I nodded as I took a nibble. "Maybe I don't need Daddy anymore."

"No, you need Daddy."

"Hi, Donovan," Jolie said loud enough that he could hear.

"He says hi back." He hadn't said it, and he wouldn't, but she didn't need to know that. "Actually, I do need something from you, D. I need to take a leave of absence."

"Of course. How long?"

I shrugged even though he couldn't see me. "Indefinitely, I think. All this is going to stir shit up, as you said, I imagine for quite a while. We'll want to lay low, and I need to give all my focus to my family."

I could tell that Jolie liked it when I said that. She grinned so hard, she glowed.

"Take the time. I'll take care of getting you replaced. You want me to tell the guys?"

I trusted the men at Reach, I did. But I also liked the idea of being off the grid. "Let's keep it just us."

"Sounds like a plan."

I caught him before he hung up. "Thank you, Donovan. I mean it. We both really appreciate this."

"Told you you still need Daddy."

The dial tone followed, and maybe I should have called him back and offered to help again with whatever troubles he was going through.

But on the other hand, there was the underneath of a shirt I needed to explore.

I TOOK one step down the stairs then immediately turned around.

"What's wrong?" Jolie stood blocking my way. Not intentionally, but the fact remained that she was there, and if I wanted to get off the stairs, I either had to go down or she needed to move.

I scratched the newly buzzed hair at the back of my neck. We'd arrived late to the day, but we'd been productive with what we had left. After returning my rental car, she'd given me a trim, then after a nap that consisted of no sleep, we'd gone to the store to buy ingredients for dinner, discussing parenting methods while strolling down the aisles.

It was reassuring that we agreed on most everything. For the rest, I'd agreed to defer to her until we were all more settled as a family, at least. Providing stability for Tate was important to both of us, second only to making sure he knew he was loved.

Jolie and I had been cooking together—something I hadn't done with someone since I'd cooked on occasion with my mother before she married Stark—when Tate had come home from his after-school activities. He'd asked what we were cooking, sniffed suspiciously at the pot of beans on the stove, then disappeared down to his room.

It had been Jolie's suggestion that this was the time to talk to him.

Having been excited about it all day, I'd eagerly taken that first step after him. Now, I was having doubts.

I considered playing tough guy for all of three seconds before I remembered I didn't want to hide my emotions from Jolie anymore. "I'm really nervous all of a sudden. What do I even say?"

She wrapped her hands around my neck. Being a stair down from her put her at my height, and that felt ridiculously comforting at the moment. "You'll figure it out."

"Will I? This conversation doesn't seem all that intuitive."

"It will be awkward. For both of you. But beginnings often are, and you can't get to a place where you're both comfortable until you get past the beginning."

"But maybe you should be there to smooth the awkwardness."

"I think you need to do this alone. Your relationship shouldn't be about me."

I groaned and dropped my head dramatically to her shoulder.

She gave a pitying laugh. "You've been through harder things."

"I don't think I have." My voice sounded muffled from her shirt sleeve.

"Seriously?" She wasn't really questioning the statement since she knew the things I'd been through and was instead questioning my attitude.

I lifted my head so she could see my pout.

She kissed it off my lips. "I'll come down in twenty minutes to check on you. How's that?"

"I'd be happier if it was fifteen."

She glanced over at the kitchen timer counting down the minutes until the ham casserole would be done in the oven. Sixteen and thirty-two seconds. "I'll pull out the food and then I'll be down."

I considered stalling for a couple of minutes, but she knew me too well. "You got this, babe. Now go get it."

Sighing, I turned back around and pushed myself to walk down. I totally had this. I'd dealt with all walks of life. I'd managed lowlifes and arrogant, rich assholes. Surely, I could get through a conversation with my son.

Though, just thinking of the term made my throat tight. I had no fucking clue how I was going to succeed in saying it.

I paused at the bottom of the stairs. Jolie had given me a quick tour earlier, which hadn't actually included Tate's room —respect for his privacy and all—but I knew where it was. Even if I hadn't been down here earlier, the steady beat of a rap song coming from behind a closed door led like aural breadcrumbs.

I stood outside long enough to recognize the artist (Eminem) and that it was a song I wasn't familiar with, suggesting it was likely one of his newer hits since I regularly boxed to his older albums and knew them inside out.

Kid had good taste in music.

The common interest gave me courage to knock.

"Yeah?" he yelled over the music.

Did that mean come in? Jolie let Tate treat his room as his own safe space. She'd never felt she had that growing up, and I respected passing that on to our son, so I called back to be sure. "Mind if I come in?"

Immediately, the music turned down, and a moment later, the door opened. "Oh, sure. Come on in."

He stepped back, and I tentatively walked in, taking in everything around me like his room was a personal guidebook to Tate Warren. "So this is your place."

Shit, I sounded like an idiot.

"Uh, it's kinda a mess. Sorry."

I hadn't been allowed a messy room when I'd lived in the Stark household, and as itchy as I got seeing the stack of discarded clothes on the gaming chair and the desk that had so many books and papers piled up that there wasn't any space to work on it, I appreciated that Jolie let the state of cleanliness be up to Tate. "Hey, it's your room."

Yeah, this was definitely awkward.

He stood watching me, probably waiting for me to hurry up and announce why I was intruding and then leave. I didn't want to rush this, though, and I wasn't going to miss this opportunity to examine all the ways his personality was expressed in his space.

I let my eyes drift to the decor now. White walls were peppered with promo posters of various PC games. I recognized several of the names, including a popular driving game that had hired Reach for their marketing campaign. Red LED lights ran along the baseboards. The bedding was black. Textbooks and his backpack were spread across the mattress, and I guessed that he did his schoolwork in his bed since the desk wasn't usable, though maybe he also used the draft table that was in the corner. There were drawings strewn across the surface, and I crossed to study them.

"You do these?" I'd expected anime figures or drawings of girls with overly large breasts, and instead I found sketches of architecturally complex buildings.

He came up next to me, and I could feel his urge to reach out and hide the drawings.

"Sorry. I should have asked." I pulled my attention away from them.

"No. I'm just not used to people looking at them. Yeah. They're mine."

Pride burst through my chest. "Really? May I?" I reached out toward one, waiting until he gave permission before picking one up to examine the modern house design. "This is really good."

He gave an embarrassed shrug. "I'm fascinated by, um, the geometry of architecture."

I'd been good at math too. The art skills, he definitely didn't get from me. "Thinking about being an architect?"

"Maybe. Lots of school." He let out a nervous laugh. "I'd rather see the world's famous structures in person than study them in a classroom."

"Me too, kid. I spent several years working jobs that took me everywhere." Fuck. I'd tell him if he asked, but I preferred to let him get to know me a little better before confessing to dealing in illegal art.

I steered the conversation back. "I know you need a degree to be an architect, but maybe you can take some time off to travel first."

"I've been thinking about that."

I handed the drawings to him, and when he set them down, he straightened all the papers on the drafting table at the same time.

I used the opportunity to put a little bit of distance between us physically and crossed to the desk on the other side of the room. I leaned against the edge and folded my arms then dropped them then stuck my hands in my pockets (what the hell were my arms supposed to do?) then cleared my throat. "So...I hear we're related."

His back was to me, and he got real still before turning around. "Yeah, Mom told me she told you."

"She did?" This was news to me. "When did she tell you?"

"She'd promised to tell me as soon as she told you, so she texted me this afternoon."

"Ah. Good mom." Yep. Fucking awkward.

Now what?

"You've known about me longer than I've known about you." I didn't know if that made this easier for him or harder, and I wasn't exactly sure what I meant by saying it out loud because he already knew that. I shifted my weight onto my hip and decided to just ask what was foremost on my mind. "Is it...weird?"

"Meeting you?" Another shrug. "I dunno. I guess. It's cool, too." He swallowed. "Is it weird for you?"

I rubbed again at my buzzed hair. "Like I said, I didn't have any inkling you existed. But there was a time that I imagined a family with Jolie so vividly that...I don't know. It's weird, but it also feels like it's just...right."

A smile fluttered quickly across his lips. "Yeah."

I let my smile stay longer, but I aimed it at my shoes. "Even feeling right, it's going to be new—for both of us. I already told you I plan to be in your lives from here on out, and I am, but I also want you to know that I don't want my relationship with your mother to have anything to do with us. I'd like to get to know you, and I don't expect that to happen all at once. But maybe we can spend time, just the two of us, sometime if that's cool?"

"That's cool."

I bit back a laugh. I supposed I'd been quiet as a teen too.

"And when you need some normality and you want to just spend time with your mom, you let me know. Or her know. Okay?"

"Okay."

"And just so you know, I'm not going to come in here and make everything different. I'm not going to try to be all 'I know best' or any of that. I don't know shit, to be honest. I'm figuring all of this out as we go."

"Okay."

"But you can come to me. We can talk things out. I'd love your help when I fuck things up—and I'm definitely going to fuck things up. Like, am I not supposed to curse? Is there a swear jar or something?"

Now he laughed. "No. Mom believes in free speech, but she does encourage more complex language choices when possible."

"Of course she does." I smiled, and this time, I met his eyes.

He smiled back.

Then again it disappeared. "Uh, so what should I call you?"

Dad. I wanted to say, *Call me Dad.*

But I didn't want to push. "Whatever you're comfortable with. You choose."

He dodged my gaze, looking everywhere but at me while he considered. "Could I...?" He wasn't bold enough to say what he wanted.

"Yes," I said, pretty sure I could guess what he was wanting. "Call me that."

"Okay. Thanks...Dad."

I would not cry. I would not cry. I would not cry.

I managed to keep my eyes from watering, but I couldn't talk. I crossed back over to him and clapped my hand on his back, an invitation for more if he chose to take it.

He did. He turned toward me, and for the first time, I hugged my son.

IT SEEMED like a blink before Jolie knocked on the door. She didn't wait for an invitation before opening the door—so she was still a mom about the privacy she granted. I couldn't help adoring her for it.

She found Tate sitting on the gaming chair—he'd tossed the laundry to the floor—and me on the bed with one of his notebooks in my lap and a pen in my hand.

"You boys doing okay?" She couldn't see Tate's half eye roll —I wasn't sure he even realized he'd done it—and another burst of warmth spread through me at the knowledge that he was enjoying his time with me enough to not want to be interrupted.

But this conversation involved her, and as devoted as I was to growing this relationship with Tate, I was still very much obsessed with his mother. "We're planning our world travels," I said. I motioned her over to me.

She came and sat next to me. "World travels?"

"Instead of college," Tate said.

"A gap year," I corrected, well aware this probably should

have been a discussion I'd had with her first. "College after that."

"Uh, do I get a say in this?" She settled her chin on my shoulder, looking at the list I'd made in the notebook.

"Of course you do. We're just talking right now." I twisted my head to kiss her cheek. "We thought it might be fun to spend some time together—all of us as a family—seeing the world before the kid leaves home."

"It was Dad's idea."

Fuck, I'd never get used to hearing that. It was overwhelming and wonderful.

"Dad," Jolie whispered so only I could hear, obviously as moved as I was.

"I know, right?"

"And these are all the places you're thinking of? Can I add to the list?" She was already taking the notebook from me before I said yes, which I was totally going to do. Truthfully, I didn't care where we went. I just wanted to be with her.

With both of them.

They were my family, and wherever they were, there was my home.

I handed her the pen.

Tate leaned forward, trying to see what she'd write. "Don't add too many!"

"Why not?" I asked.

At the same time, Jolie said, "We can vote for where we want to go most."

"But I want to go so many places. I need to see the Parthenon in Greece. And the Taj Mahal in India. And La Sagrada Familia in Spain. And Hagia Sophia in Turkey."

I was impressed. I couldn't name half of the buildings my son had mentioned let alone where they were.

"We'll use ranked choice voting," Jolie said, adding the Galapagos Islands and Myanmar to the already long list.

"Or we just go to all of them," I suggested. "We'll have a year."

"Really?" This from Jolie.

"We're just dreaming," Tate said. "I know a trip like that would be expensive as hell."

I'd been a dad for a little more than a day, and I already knew the feeling of wanting my teenage son to think I was cool. I leaned forward, as if I was about to admit a secret. "This might be a good time to tell you, Tate—I'm loaded."

His eyes went wide, and he looked to his mother for confirmation.

Her nod felt reluctant. "It doesn't mean anything changes. We're not spoiling you. Are we, Cade?"

I wasn't sure I could commit to that. If I looked at her, she'd know.

"Cade!" She slapped my shoulder when I wouldn't meet her eyes.

"Okay, okay. We're not spoiling you. But college is paid for, and we are going on a world trip where I'm going to spoil you." I directed this *you* to her. "And Tate's invited to come along." I winked at him.

He winked back.

She pretended to deliberate, but she wasn't fooling anyone. She knew we deserved happiness after everything we'd been through. We deserved to be spoiled for the rest of time. "All right. I'll let you spoil me."

I kissed her quickly, which elicited a groan of annoyance from Tate, but his smile said he wasn't *that* annoyed.

"So let's see where we're going." I pulled the notebook back from my wife-to-be—there'd have to be an engagement and a wedding thrown in all of our plans at some point, but I wasn't worried about it too much. It would happen. "We have Scotland, Paris, Greece, Turkey, Spain, Rome, India, Japan—I already have an apartment in Tokyo, so we can stay a while; there's so much I want to show you there—the Galapagos Islands, and Myanmar."

"And Iceland," Jolie added enthusiastically.

"And Iceland." I wrote it down, about to burst. Was it possible to hold this much joy inside? Even when we'd dreamed about a future together as kids, I'd never been this happy. It was an entirely different thing to anticipate something that I knew would happen than something that I hoped would happen.

And I knew our trip would happen.

Or if it didn't, it would be because we chose something else that was better. I had no doubts. Nothing stood in our way of taking everything we reached for. A glance at Jolie said she was bursting with the same joy.

"Fucking good itinerary there." I ignored Jolie's frown at the swearing and looked to Tate. "How does it sound to you?"

He took the words right out of my mouth. "Sounds wild."

EPILOGUE

CADE

Eighteen months later

Jolie jumped and grabbed on to me as the cork came out with a loud pop.

"I wasn't expecting that," she said as laughter rippled through our group.

"I wasn't either." Weston held the bottle away from him, though the champagne was already dripping down his sleeve, so I didn't really see the point. "Guess it got shaken up in the process of opening it."

"My carpet appreciates it," Donovan said with smug sarcasm. "How about I open the next one?"

"I got you, I got you." Weston's wife, Elizabeth, came to the rescue carrying two flutes. She positioned one under the nozzle as he poured then replaced it with another when she handed off the first to Jolie.

Sabrina came up behind her with more flutes, and between the three of them, we soon all had glasses in hand except Tate.

Elizabeth held the last flute in front of him and looked toward us. "Is this okay?"

Tate raised a hopeful brow, and Jolie frowned.

"Come on. We're celebrating," I said to my fiancée.

"Which is a fine excuse for your drinking, not for our eighteen-year-old." Jolie had been my rock when I'd decided to cut back on alcohol except for wine at dinner, for a myriad of reasons—health and being a present parent topped the list.

"He's going to be able to legally drink tomorrow when we're in France."

"But today, we're still in New York." God, she was adorable when she was ridiculous. As if Tate hadn't snuck a sip or two from our wine glasses in the past.

I might have even let him have one of her margarita coolers when she was out of town last spring to deal with the final sale of the school property to a rehabilitation organization for women and children who had been rescued victims of human trafficking. Did she really think I'd been the one to dig into her stash?

"Ah, for Pete's sake, let the kid drink." Donovan swiped the drink from Elizabeth's hand and gave it to Tate then raised his own glass in the air before anyone could object. "To safe and adventurous travels."

"Thank you," Weston said, as if the toast was meant for him, which he probably assumed it was.

Jolie sighed, but she raised her glass with everyone else. "Here, here!"

Clinking glasses and cheers followed, and when everyone

drank, Tate made a big show of being disgusted with the taste for his mother's sake but not so disgusted that he relinquished the glass. In my arms, Devyn stiffened at the commotion.

"Hey, baby bird. Did that startle you?" I bent my face down to reassure my seven-month-old daughter. As soon as she saw my grin, she gave me one of her own.

"Her smile kills me," Sabrina cooed. "Those two little teeth are so cute."

Jolie reached over to straighten her jumper. "Not so cute when she's biting on my breast, but yeah. We like her."

Fuck yeah, we liked her.

For so long in my life, I'd believed the best I could be had passed. Once upon a time, I'd been the boy Julianna Stark had loved, and nothing could top that.

Then I met my son, and the whole universe shifted. Being his father had become my gravity. It held me in place and was such an essential part of my reality, I couldn't comprehend anymore that I'd once existed without him.

I loved him and his mother with every cell in my body, and when Jolie got pregnant a few short months after our reunion, I'd been surprised to find there was room inside me to love more.

The first time I'd held her, I thought I was going to explode.

If sobbing like a baby counted as such, then I did explode. One of the happiest days of my life, and there'd been plenty of those in the eighteen months since I'd taken a leave from Reach.

Including tonight, celebrating Tate's recent graduation with friends before we took off on our year-long trip around the world.

"I can't believe you're traveling with an infant," Elizabeth said.

I looked up to find her so baffled she was shaking her head. I supposed it was to be expected from a woman who was celebrating her babymoon sans baby in her womb. To be fair, she was the heiress to a giant media company and loved her career. So instead of taking time off to have a baby on their own, Weston and Elizabeth had asked the mother of Weston's son from a previous relationship—if a one-night stand could be called a relationship—to surrogate for them.

If it worked for them, who was I to have an opinion?

"We have a nanny traveling with us," Jolie said.

"An old lady nanny," Tate added. "I still say we should have hired the twenty-five-year-old."

"You have a girlfriend," his mother reminded him.

"We're on a break," he reminded her.

Having lost so much time together, it was difficult for Jol and me to understand Tate and his girlfriend wanting to spend any time apart. Ironically, he'd credited our relationship as the inspiration. *True love will still be there when we get back to it*, he'd said. *If it's not, then it's not true love.*

He was a wise one. I wasn't jerking his chain whenever I told him I looked up to him.

"Anyway." Jolie turned her attention back to Elizabeth. "Even with the nanny, we intend to take Devyn with us as much as possible."

"We're a real together sort of family." If I sounded proud of the fact, I was.

Weston moved over to join the conversation with a four-year-old wrapped around his leg like that was everyday for him. "So we've discovered. So tight-knit you didn't tell anyone where you were for more than a year and a half." He paused for dramatic effect. "Oh, wait. I mean since you didn't tell me where you were."

Donovan and I exchanged a glance. He'd taken me seriously when I'd asked him to keep our lives hush-hush. The rest of the firm had been told nothing except that I'd been on sabbatical. Weston had only been caught up on the events of my life in the last hour over dinner hosted at Donovan's. He'd been playing hurt ever since.

I stuck my tongue out at Sebastian—the four-year-old wrapped around Weston's leg—before responding. "Look, I'm sorry I didn't tell you. There was a lot of media—"

"So much media," Sabrina agreed.

"We even covered it in the European markets," Elizabeth added.

"And we were trying to maintain some normalcy." Too much of our lives had been not normal. Choosing to drop off the grid had been one of the best choices I'd ever made.

"I get it," Weston said in a tone that said he really didn't. "I just thought we were closer than that, you know? You came all the way from Tokyo for my wedding—and it hadn't even been a legit wedding."

"He didn't really come for your wedding," Donovan said, flat-toned.

Weston went on as if he hadn't heard the interruption. "At least you're here tonight. We only get to the States once a year, at most. It was really great of you to come to New York to see us."

"He didn't really come to New York to see you." Donovan again.

I only somewhat successfully bit back a smile. "Wouldn't

have missed tonight for the world." Because it was the first leg of our trip, not because of Weston. I hadn't even known he'd be in town when I'd told Donovan we'd be there.

Weston appeared somewhat mollified. "Is it safe to assume we'll get an invitation to your wedding?"

Jolie and I looked at each other. We still hadn't decided if we were going to do something big or something quiet. Truth was that we hadn't spent any time at all planning the event. When she'd found out she was pregnant, she'd wanted to wait until after the baby was born. And then we were so busy planning the trip, we decided to push it until after that.

At least, she was wearing a ring now. I'd officially popped the question on Valentine's Day with a gorgeous diamond ring surrounded by Tate and Devyn's birthstones (garnet and topaz). As far as we were concerned, that was more ceremony than we needed, but the idea of celebrating with friends did have its appeal.

"When we get around to figuring out what that will look like, sure," I said.

Sabrina linked her arm through Donovan's. "Watch what you're saying in present company. Donovan will surprise you with a wedding if you're not careful."

Everyone laughed because it was true.

"He throws good weddings," Elizabeth said.

I groaned. "Please, don't encourage him."

"I don't know. Seems sort of fitting since he's practically responsible for you being together. According to him, anyway." Sometimes Weston was clueless, but sometimes I thought he stirred shit on purpose.

I sent a pointed glare in Donovan's direction. "Oh, is that right?"

"I didn't say it in quite so many words. But while we're on the topic, how about you show them?"

I didn't have to ask what Donovan meant.

Rolling my eyes, I finished off my champagne in a single gulp and handed the flute to the asshole before offering Devyn to whoever volunteered.

"I got her." Tate had been as excited as we were to add her to our family. Sometimes I wondered if he was more of a third parent than a brother. I worried about him eventually going away to college. It was going to break her heart.

Okay, it was going to break my heart.

Which was why I wasn't thinking about it until I had to.

With my hands free, I loosened my belt and lifted up my button-down so I could display **I love D** tattooed on my right hip.

Elizabeth's eyes went gleefully wide, and she covered her mouth.

Weston didn't bother hiding his laugh at all. "Seriously, Cade? You let him put that on you permanently?"

"Well, I didn't ink it on him myself," Donovan said, obviously pleased with himself despite the fact.

"A bet's a bet," I said. "But the joke's on him." I pulled my pants down a bit so everyone could see what I'd had added to the tattoo since Donovan had last seen it—**EVYN.**

"I love Devyn," Weston read out loud.

"You motherfucker," Donovan muttered. "I call that cheating."

"I call it genius." Sabrina didn't even look sorry when her husband threw her a look. Honestly, the whole exchange seemed like foreplay.

I definitely didn't want to think about that.

"I got two other new tattoos when I had that one done." I showed everyone the open birdcage on the left lower side of my back that matched Jolie's tattoo and then rolled up my sleeve to show off the house that had been an original design. "Tate did that one."

"He's really good."

I puffed up from Elizabeth's praise as if she'd been praising me and glanced over at Tate for his reaction. He was plopped on the ground now, trying to draw on his iPad while Devyn crawled back and forth over his stretched-out legs, and though he didn't look up, the color in his cheeks said he'd heard the compliment.

The kid was too humble for his own good. I would have boasted more if he hadn't been present. There was still a chance I'd boast more before the night was over.

"Yeah, yeah, we know," Donovan pretended to grumble. "You're a family man now. And I'd had such high hopes for you."

I shot him a glare.

Then decided on another tactic. If he was going to poke, it was only fair that I poke back. "And how about you, D? You're married now. You planning any mini Kincaids?"

She made it seem casual, but Sabrina chose that moment to step away from her husband and crouch down by Tate to see what he was drawing.

Weston bent down to pick up Devyn who had taken Tate's distraction as an opportunity to reach for the first editions on Donovan's bookshelf. "You're going to have to babyproof, if you are."

"You know what? Mind your own business," Donovan said.

Yes, we definitely laughed.

"That's rich coming from you," I said.

"I have no idea what you're talking about. How about I break open another bottle?"

It was a change of subject if I'd ever seen one, and I might have pushed him on it if it was the old days, when it was just the two of us. When all we had of the women we loved were wild memories and deep regrets.

That wasn't us anymore.

Thank God.

I wrapped an arm around Jolie's waist and pulled her to me while Donovan worked on opening the next bottle. "You happy?" I asked.

"Impossibly."

And when Donovan handed me my replenished glass, I didn't need an excuse to celebrate. My impossibly happy life was reason enough.

———

Stay tuned for the next Dirty Universe installment

Kincaid

Not just a retelling.

More than an epilogue.
Past and present weave together in Donovan's point of view
for the next chapter in Donovan and Sabrina's life.
Coming late 2022

If you're not caught up on the Dirty Universe, start with Dirty Filthy Rich Men or check out the reading order on laurelinpaige.com

A NOTE FROM THE AUTHOR AND ACKNOWLEDGMENTS

Welp.

I said this was the last trilogy in the Dirty Universe. Then, when I was mid through this final book, I started thinking more about what I wanted to write next. I get an email or message at least once a week asking for another Donovan book, and when I tried to imagine him in the epilogue for Wild Heart—because if this was really the finale, we had to see where everyone was—I realized I couldn't just slap Donovan and Sabrina with a baby on the way and call it quits. Their relationship is too complex for me to imagine what that would look like without a thorough exploration.

So there will be more of the Dirty.

But that's getting ahead of myself. Now is about Cade and Jolie. I always knew their story was going to be more heart wrenching than sexy (though I hope it's sexy too), and I knew they were going to wreck me to write, and I am so grateful that I had such amazing people to support me while I did.

Instead of going through and saying who did what and what position they have in my team/bubble/life, I'm just going to dump a bunch of names here, in no particular order. Names of people who have been extremely important to me this last year and always:

Candi Kane, Melissa Gaston, Roxie Madar, Kayti McGee, Sarah Piechuta, Amy Vox Libris, Erica Russikoff, Michele Ficht, Kimberly Ruiz, Liz Berry, Brandie Coonis, Ann R. Jones, Rebecca Friedman, Kim Gilmour, Andi Arndt, Sebastian York, Lauren Blakely, CD Reiss, Melanie Harlow, Orion Allison, Open Cathedral, my littles (who aren't so little) and the adulters (who only sort of adult) in my household, and the Higher Power who leads me through all the chaos.

Last but not least, thank you dear readers who pick up the book time after time after time. If I were to fill a book with enough words to express my gratitude, it would never be finished.

XO,

Laurelin

PAIGE PRESS

Paige Press isn't just Laurelin Paige anymore...

Laurelin Paige has expanded her publishing company to bring readers even more hot romances.

Sign up for our newsletter to get the latest news about our releases and receive a free book from one of our amazing authors:

Stella Gray
CD Reiss
Jenna Scott
Raven Jayne
JD Hawkins
Poppy Dunne
Lia Hunt

ABOUT LAURELIN PAIGE

With millions of books sold, Laurelin Paige is the NY Times, Wall Street Journal, and USA Today Bestselling Author of the Fixed Trilogy. She's a sucker for a good romance and gets giddy anytime there's kissing, much to the embarrassment of her three daughters. Her husband doesn't seem to complain, however. When she isn't reading or writing sexy stories, she's probably singing, watching shows like Killing Eve, Letterkenny, and Discovery of Witches, or dreaming of Michael Fassbender. She's also a proud member of Mensa International though she doesn't do anything with the organization except use it as material for her bio.

www.laurelinpaige.com
laurelinpaigeauthor@gmail.com